**"You're a traitor!" Ladd snapped at Clint.**

They were facing Hickok, the six of them, when suddenly Clint had moved away and stood alongside their intended victim.

"Being a traitor's better than being a coward," Clint replied. "And six against one makes for six cowards."

"How do you feel about five against two?" Hickok asked this stranger at his side.

Clint shrugged. "Sounds like even odds to me."

Hickok smiled. "You and I have to play poker, my friend!"

Ladd and the others were fanning out. Clint looked toward the two men on the left, Hickok the two on the right. "What about the one in the middle?" Hickok asked.

"I've got ten dollars that says I work my way to him before you do."

"You're cocky," Hickok laughed, "but you're on!"

Don't miss any of the lusty, hard-riding action in the
Charter Western series, THE GUNSMITH

And coming next month:
THE GUNSMITH #51: DESERT HELL

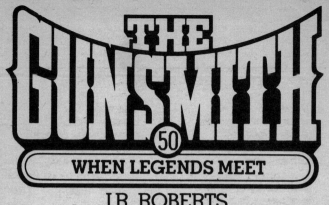

# THE GUNSMITH

## 50

## WHEN LEGENDS MEET

### J.R. ROBERTS

CHARTER BOOKS, NEW YORK

THE GUNSMITH #50: WHEN LEGENDS MEET

A Charter Book/published by arrangement with
the author

PRINTING HISTORY
Charter edition/February 1986

ISBN: 0-441-30954-2

Charter Books arc published by The Berkley Publishing Group,
200 Madison Avenue, New York, New York 10016.
PRINTED IN THE UNITED STATES OF AMERICA

*To Ed Gorman,*
*Good Writer, Good Critic, Good Friend,*
*not necessarily in that order . . .*

*and to all the Gunsmith readers who*
*have kept us going.*
*THANKS!*

# PROLOGUE

It was a story that, as far as Rick Hartman knew, had never been told before. Tonight, he thought he had the Gunsmith in the right mood to tell it, a melancholy mood brought on in large part by a lot of Hartman's best whiskey and an incident that had occurred earlier that day.

As was usually the case when Clint Adams returned to Labyrinth, Texas, from his travels, he found that Rick Hartman had hired some new women in his saloon. Being a saloon girl was a temporary job. Usually the women worked until they saved up enough money to move to the next town.

In this instance, Rick had hired two women—one a tall, willowy brunette and the other a shorter, somewhat more buxom redhead who, if she were not careful, could easily have become chunky.

Clint was in his hotel room with the redhead, Gloria Lyons, enjoying the bountiful fruits of her body when there was a knock at the door.

"What?" he called out irritably, lifting his head from between her full breasts. He kept his fingers working between her legs, though, drawing her body as taut as a guitar string ready to snap.

"Uh, there's a man downstairs who wants to see you, Mr. Adams," the desk clerk called out from the hall.

"What about?"

"I didn't ask him that."

He looked down at Gloria's face. Her eyes were glazed and she bit her lip as she approached her orgasm. He became acutely aware of his own need as his rigid penis throbbed painfully.

"I need you here," she whispered.

"Tell him to wait!" he shouted, and then lowered his mouth to her nipples, which were already distended. He suckled them until she began to moan uncontrollably. He had intended to go more slowly, tasting her all over, but now he slid onto her, prodding her with the head of his cock and then, clutching her ample buttocks tightly in his hands, he punched home.

He dressed and told Gloria to wait for him to come back.

"I'm not going anywhere," she said, stretching luxuriously, lifting her full breasts high. It was not so much that Clint preferred her to the willowy brunette. It was just that he had decided to try her first. It was afternoon, and he had an evening date with the other woman, Carrie Nelson.

After strapping on his gun, he left the room and walked to the stairs that led to the lobby. As he descended the stairs, a man looked up from a bench against the wall and stood. He was dressed in city clothes, and Clint figured that he had probably come from the east, either New York or Chicago or some other large city.

Clint's hackles rose as he approached the man because there was something unpleasantly familiar about him.

"Mr. Adams?" the man asked somewhat eagerly.

"That's right."

"My name is Nichols, sir, Andrew Nichols."

Clint froze. He studied the man, who appeared to be in his late twenties, and realized now why he had looked so familiar to him.

"Does the name mean anything to you?"

"Should it?"

"You knew my father, sir, Colonel George Ward Nichols. He wrote some articles about you, oh, some fifteen years or so ago."

"I remember," Clint said coldly.

"Good, I was hoping you would. You see, I'm a writer, too, and I work for a Chicago paper. My editor and I thought it would be a fine idea to look you up fifteen years later and interview you for a series of articles. There has been much written about you since my father's stories about you and Wild Bill Hickok sort of made you both famous, but there's been nothing in depth about you for quite some time. So, sir, I was wondering if you—"

"Mr. Nichols," Clint said evenly, "if I were you, I'd take the next stage out of Labyrinth and head back to Chicago where you belong."

Nichols frowned and said, "I'm afraid I don't understand."

"I'll explain it to you," Clint said. "I didn't want any articles or stories written about me fifteen years ago, I didn't want any damn dime novels written about me as they were last year, and I don't want any damned interviews done now. Is that clear enough?"

"I still don't understand."

"Your father's articles may have started me on the road to becoming famous, Mr. Nichols, and in doing so they made my life hell to live."

"But—"

"He made me a target for every two-bit cowboy who thought he knew how to use a gun," Clint said, prodding the young Mr. Nichols's chest with a stiffened forefinger. "You're looking to stir things up again for me, and believe me, I don't need it. Get out of town!" he finished, emphasizing each word by poking the man in the chest forcefully.

Nichols started to open his mouth to reply, but something in the Gunsmith's eyes stopped him.

"I'm sorry to have bothered you, sir," Nichols said, starting for the door.

"Nichols," Clint called.

"Yes?" the man asked, turning.

"What ever happened to your father?"

"He died five years ago."

Clint had returned to Gloria and taken his anger out on her, channeling it into passion. Later, he had done the same to Carrie, the brunette. He effectively wore both women out, and then he had gone to Rick's and started drinking.

Hartman knew that the Gunsmith was still grieving over Wild Bill Hickok's death, even after all this time. It was the kind of grief felt at the loss of a loved one—in this case, Hickok had been like a brother. Young Nichols from Chicago had brought the grief and thoughts of the past bubbling to the surface.

As far as Hartman knew, Clint Adams had no living relatives and grieved for none of them. Of course, there was a woman he still grieved for, Joanna Morgan, and although that grief was different from what Clint felt for Hickok, it was in some ways much the same.

Clint Adams had lost the only two people he ever really cared deeply about. Hartman had no trouble understanding the grief for his woman. He knew that story well enough, but the story of Clint's friendship with Hickok was one he had never heard. Clint had always told him, "Another time, Rick. Some other time," when he touched on the subject.

Tonight, however, Hartman was playing it smart. Clint seemed to be drifting toward that story of his own accord, and Rick was simply watching and waiting for the right moment.

And then it came.

"Yeah," Clint was saying, "Ole Bill was something. Why when we first met . . ." Clint trailed off and Rick leaned forward in anticipation.

"Ah, you can tell me that story some other time, Clint," he said, pouring his drunken friend another drink. "Have a drink and forget about all of that."

It was after hours and they were the only two people in Rick's Place, Hartman's saloon in Labyrinth, Texas.

He looked at Clint to see what effect, if any, his words were having on him, but the Gunsmith was staring off into space with a bemused look on his face.

"Hey, come on," Hartman said, jostling his friend's arm, "you're drifting away on me."

Clint's eyes attempted to focus on Hartman and he said, "Uh, I was just thinking . . ."

His heart beating with anticipation Rick Hartman leaned forward even more and asked, "About what?"

And the Gunsmith began to speak . . .

# ONE

The town was Springfield, Missouri. The Civil War had ended only months before, and Clint Adams was still carrying much of the pay he'd received from his hitch with the Union army. He'd saved his money and, upon receiving his honorable discharge, decided to spend it slowly and wisely—on fast women and wise cards.

In his late twenties, Clint Adams was a tall, ramrod straight man, slim but tautly muscled. He was riding a big roan he called Jake, and on his hip was a conventional, single-action, solid frame Colt. In his saddlebag was a gun he was tinkering with, a Colt-style gun he had pieced together and was trying to convert to double-action. The result would be a gun that was easy to break down and keep clean and that would fire without having to be cocked first. He had read something about a gun like that being on display in Europe and had been trying to build himself one ever since. He just about had it, now, and would probably test it in Springfield.

He topped a rise and pulled Jake to a halt, looking down at the sprawling town of Springfield. New towns excited the young man because he didn't know what they held in store for him. A poker game, yes; women, certainly; but what after that?

Only one way to find out.

"Hickok, you're going about this the wrong way," Ed Blaine said to James Butler Hickok. Some men called him

Wild Bill, although Blaine didn't know why and didn't have the nerve to ask.

"What do you mean?" Hickok asked. He was a tall, handsome man in his late twenties with a carefully cared for mustache and beard and long, chestnut hair that hung past his shoulders. Women marveled at his broad shoulders, and men feared the twin Colts he wore tucked into the waistband of his trousers, disdaining hip holsters and gunbelts.

"You want to be marshal, don't you?"

"Sure."

"Then you shouldn't be carrying on with another man's woman."

"Jamie is Dave Tutt's sister," Hickok reminded the man who was handling his campaign for marshal, "not his woman. You know that."

"Yeah, but Tutt acts like she's his woman, jealous and protective and all." Blaine allowed himself a brief comment on that, "An unhealthy situation, that." Then he returned to the subject at hand. "Besides, I'm not so sure you really want her for herself, anyway."

They were in Hickok's hotel room, and the candidate clad in his usual buckskins, placed his hat on his head at a rakish angle and said, "What do you mean?"

"Well, I know how you feel about Tutt and Jim Courtwright, how you think they betrayed you during the war and all."

"I don't think, Ed," Hickok said forcefully, his eyes turning cold. "I know."

"Well, then, all the more reason you shouldn't go after the man's sister," Blaine explained. "I don't know why you insist on it."

Hickok smiled, a twinkle abruptly melting the ice of his eyes, and said, "Hell, she's a pretty little thing."

Blaine opened his mouth to argue, but he couldn't. Jamie

Tutt was extraordinarily pretty, probably the prettiest woman in town.

"I can't argue that."

"Then stop arguing at all and do what you're supposed to do. Get me elected."

"All right, all right," Blaine said, standing up from the bed, "I'll do my job, but you sure as hell don't make it an easy one to do."

Hickok looked at the short, portly former newspaperman and said, "If it was easy, I wouldn't need your help doing it, would I?"


In a small, wood-frame house at the other end of town, Dave Tutt shouted, "I won't have it!"

Jamie Tutt tugged at the bodice of her dress to make sure it fit properly and then turned away from the mirror to face her brother and said, "Don't shout at me like that, David."

Jamie was a pretty, auburn-haired young woman, barely twenty years of age. She was about five feet four and filled her dress out in a womanly fashion that made her brother frown with concern. She was the most sought after young woman in town, the young men attracted to her in droves and repelled by her brutish brother.

Dave Tutt, her brother, was more than ten years older, a big, hulking man with a head of shaggy brown hair and huge, sloping shoulders. Their parents had died seven years earlier, leaving Dave Tutt with a budding, curious teenage girl to care for, and it hadn't gotten any easier as she got older.

"I won't have my sister carrying on with a cheap, fancy-dressing gunman!"

"Don't talk about James like that," she said, turning and scolding her brother with a stamp of her foot. When she was angry, she looked even prettier, the third person in the room observed.

"Jamie," Dave Tutt said, his tone almost pleading, "he's only seeing you to get to me. Can't you understand that?"

"No," Jamie said, "I don't believe that about James, and I resent you saying it. Do you think I'm not attractive enough to get a man on my own?"

"No, damn it, I didn't mean that," Tutt said. He knew well how attractive his sister was—too damned attractive, for his money. God, how he sometimes wished his parents had given birth to a homely girl.

Seated, in a corner Jim Courtwright watched brother and sister with an amused smile. Dave Tutt spent half his days arguing with the girl, and Courtwright could not remember him ever having won.

"Jamie—"

"You're not my father, David Tutt!"

"I'm as good as—"

"Pa would see James Hickok for what he is," Jamie shot back, "a gentleman. You see him as . . . as some sort of competition! It's absurd!"

"I don't know what that means!" Dave Tutt replied in exasperation.

"Absurd means silly," Courtwright chimed in.

"You're just as bad as he is," Jamie said, looking at the seated man, who was older than both of them.

"I didn't say anything."

"No, but you've got it in for Jim Hickok, too, I can tell."

"Jamie—" Dave tried again, but he wasn't going to get anywhere near winning this argument.

"I'm going out, Dave," she said. "I'll see you later for dinner."

"Jamie—" he said again, but she turned on her heel, picked up her bag, and walked out of the house.

Tutt turned to Courtwright, held his hands out helplessly, and said, "I can't win!"

Courtwright smiled and said, "Why should today be different from any other day?"

On his way to Springfield at this time was Colonel George Ward Nichols of *Harper's Weekly*. He was in search of an exciting gunman or outlaw to write up to boost the circulation. He felt that the readers in the east were ripe for stories about a man whose abilities with a gun were legendary, the kind of stories that would add spice to their humdrum little lives.

All he had to do was find the right man.

Also on her way to the town of Springfield, Missouri—to add more flame to an already boiling pot, as it were—was Susannah Moore, a stunning, buxom blonde who was an old acquaintance of James Hickok's. Miss Moore's part, essentially, would be as the fuse to the dynamite.

Unintentionally, of course.

Clint Adams was unaware, as he rode down Springfield's main street, that he was to play an integral part in the lives of all of these people and that he would come out of Springfield a much better known man than he had gone in.

His legend would begin here, a legend that would go on for years and would very probably outlive him.

# TWO

Clint Adams found the Springfield livery and placed his roan in the liveryman's hands. Toting his saddlebags and Henry rifle he made his way to a hotel, passing on the way a tall, well-dressed man with long brown hair and steely eyes. The man didn't seem to notice him, yet Clint had the feeling that he had been studied, catalogued, and filed away for later reference—much the same thing, in fact, that he had done to the other man. He turned and regarded the man a moment more, long enough to determine that he was going inside the livery.

At the Springfield Hotel he got a room and a bath and directions to the nearest saloon, all of which he made good use of.

Hickok, having rented a buckboard from the saloon, picked up Jamie Tutt and drove both of them out to a small lake a few miles outside of town. There they spread a blanket, sat, and ate a lunch Jamie had purchased from a café.

"Dave is giving me trouble again," she said.

"About me?"

"Yes."

Hickok touched her arm and said, "Jamie, maybe we'd better stop seeing each other—for your sake."

"That's silly," she said, brushing the suggestion away. "I can handle Dave."

13

"I know, but—"

She leaned forward and silenced him with a perfunctory kiss on the mouth. "I won't hear of it, James Hickok."

"You're quite a gal."

"Yes," she said, grinning, "I know."

She was indeed quite a gal, but Hickok couldn't quite dispose of the thought that maybe Ed Blaine was right, maybe he was only seeing her to get at Dave Tutt.

He just wasn't sure, but as he reached for her and slid her dress from her shoulders, baring her firm, young breasts and palming them, he knew that even if that was a reason, there were others . . .

At the Deadline Saloon, Clint Adams was nursing a beer when he became privy—quite innocently—to a conversation at the next table.

There was a huge, hulking man sitting with three other men who seemed to be drifters, and they appeared to be striking some kind of bargain.

"Make it look good," he heard the big man say, passing some money to one man who would, presumably, share with the others.

"How bad you want him hurt?" the man asked.

"As bad as possible."

"You mean like . . . for good?" one of the others said, and Clint could see in that man's eyes that the suggestion did not sit well with him.

"There's more money where that came from," the big man said and that seemed to make the idea sit better in the other man's mind easily enough.

"All right," the man who had accepted the money agreed.

"And get more men."

"The three of us can handle it—" one of the men began.

But the big man cut him off. ''This bastard is as good with a gun as any man I've ever seen,'' he told them. ''Get more men.''

''If he's that fast—'' one of the others started.

''There's more money,'' the big man said, and again those were the magic words.

''What have you got against this fella, anyway?'' one of them asked.

''That you ain't getting paid to know,'' the big man said, standing up. His eyes flicked over Clint at the next table, assessed him, and then looked away. ''I'll see you when the job's done,'' the man told the drifters, and then he left the saloon.

Nice, friendly town, Clint thought.

''What did you do?'' Jim Courtwright asked when Dave Tutt met him at Springfield's other saloon, Green Branch.

''What I had to do,'' Tutt said, sitting down and picking up Courtwright's beer.

''Get your own,'' Courtwright said as Tutt drank from it, but he made no move to reclaim the mug.

''I'm taking care of Wild Bill Hickok once and for all,'' Dave Tutt said, setting the half-empty mug back down on the table.

''You're making a mistake,'' Courtwright said, shaking his head.

''Jim, you know as well as I do that if Hickok gets elected marshal this town ain't gonna be fit for either of us to live in.''

''There are other ways.''

''Not for me,'' Tutt said, shaking his head. ''If I don't get him first—if we don't get him—then he's gonna get us and that ain't something I want to happen.''

Courtwright frowned at first, but against his better judgment, he was starting to believe that maybe the other man was right.

"You'll see," Tutt said, finishing the beer. "Why don't you get us two more?" he suggested.

"Is one for me?" Courtwright asked, but he got up and walked to the bar.

When he returned with the two beers, Tutt said, "You and I will be right here when it happens, so there won't be no question about us being involved."

"I hope not," Courtwright said, and he did not point out that, technically, he wasn't involved.

That little fact could always come in handy later on—if need be.

# THREE

After the big, hulking man had left the saloon, two of the other men got up and left while the third—the one who had been given the money—stayed put. Clint thought it over a moment, then picked up his beer and moved to join the other man at his table.

"Mind if I join you?"

The man looked at him, frowning, and said, "Yeah, I do."

"Come on, now, be friendly," Clint said. "My name is Jake," he told the man, taking the name of his horse for this little bit of deception.

"So?"

"I was sitting at the next table there and couldn't help but hear your conversation. Seems to me you've taken on a job that needs a few more men."

"Mister, this ain't none of your affair—"

"Okay, look," Clint said, sliding his chair back to get up, "I'm going back to my own table. When your friends come back, just remember me if you find you need another man, huh? I could use the extra money."

The man started to speak, but Clint stood up and walked back to his own table. The other man stared at him for a moment, then turned his attention to his own beer.

It took about a half hour for the other two men to return,

and from the heated discussion and shaking of heads, Clint thought he knew what the problem was.

The man he had spoken to turned in his chair to look at him and then spoke to the other men briefly before getting up and walking to Clint's table.

The man was in his forties, beefy, and badly in need of a bath and a shave.

"Mind if I join you?"

"Only if it doesn't mean money," Clint replied.

The man sat and said, "My name's Ladd. You were right; we've got a job that we feel we can handle, but the man who's paying us says we'll need six men. We've only got five. The job is—"

"I know what the job is," Clint said. "What I want to know is how much money is involved."

"A lot," Ladd said. "We've been promised fifty dollars a piece."

It was all Clint could do not to laugh. To these drifters, fifty dollars each was all the money in the world. "Fifty dollars to kill a man," Clint said, rubbing his jaw.

"Good money, huh? And easy, with six of us."

"All right," Clint said. "I'm with you. When do we do this?"

"According to the liveryman he'll come riding down the main street any time now. He'll be with a girl, but she's not important."

"We don't have to kill her?" Clint asked, feigning surprise.

"Not that I know of, but if we did, we'd want more money."

"Of course."

"Why don't you come and join us at our table. The other men will be along soon."

"Uh, I think I'll just stay here and finish my beer. I'll be ready when you give the word."

The man hesitated a moment, then said, "All right, Jake. Here's ten dollars, on account."

Clint accepted the money and tucked it away. Ladd returned to his table, and when the other two men showed up, he handed out ten dollars to each.

All five of the men seated at the other table were dressed in worn trail clothes, wearing equally worn gunbelts; they were all in need of baths and a shave.

Clint had more than one reason for not wanting to share a table with them.

One of the men abruptly got up and walked to the doors, presumably to keep watch for their intended target. Clint wondered what the poor man had done to deserve this.

When Hickok turned the buckboard into the main street of Springfield, he immediately sensed that something was amiss. He pulled the horse to a stop.

"What's wrong, James?" Jamie asked.

"The street's empty for this time of day, don't you think?"

She looked at the street and frowned. "Why, yes, it does seem empty. What does it mean?"

"An empty street usually means trouble."

"Why do you say that?"

"People have a way of sensing trouble, Jamie, and they tend to stay off the street until it's over."

"What kind of trouble?"

"That's what we're going to find out," he said, flicking the reins and starting the horse forward again.

"Here he comes," the man at the door announced.

"Jake," Ladd said, rising with his other men.

"I'm coming," Clint said, standing up.

He followed the other men out the door, and as they all spread out on the walk, Clint saw that their intended target was riding down the street on a buckboard with a girl next to him. He recognized the man.

It was the man he had passed on his way to his hotel.

"Jesus," Jim Courtwright said.

He was standing at the window of the Green Branch saloon and Tutt, who was seated, looked up and asked, "What's wrong?"

"Do you know that Jamie is with Hickok?"

"No, why?"

"You better come over here."

Tutt walked to the window and peered out. What he saw froze his blood. The six men he had hired were fanned out in front of Hickok's buckboard, and on the seat next to him was Tutt's sister, Jamie.

"Damn it," he snapped. "Those fools are going to brace him with Jamie right there."

He started for the door, but Courtwright grabbed his arm, holding him back.

"You want the whole town to know that you hired six men to gun Hickok?"

"But Jamie—"

"Look," Courtwright said, "Hickok's smart enough to get her out of his way."

As they watched, Hickok stepped down, helped Jamie down, and then pushed her away from him. She stepped to the walk and took cover in the doorway of a store. At that moment, a stagecoach pulled in and people began to alight and become aware of the impending trouble. They also mounted the walk to find cover.

"Thank God," Tutt breathed, moving away from the door to the window again.

"Now let's watch," Courtwright said.

"What the hell—" Tutt said.

As they continued to watch, one of the six men who were facing Hickok suddenly moved away from his five companions and stood alongside Hickok.

"What the hell is going on?"

"Let's just watch and find out."

"What's your story?" Hickok asked Clint as he moved alongside the intended victim.

"I was just minding my own business when I heard there was fifty dollars on someone's head. I thought I'd cut myself in and see if the poor soul needed any help when the time came."

"You in the habit of cutting yourself in on someone else's trouble?"

"After today," Clint replied, "maybe not anymore."

"You traitor!" Ladd snapped.

"That's always better than being a coward," Clint said, "and six against one makes for six cowards."

"How do you feel about five against two?" Hickok asked the stranger who appeared to be allying himself with him.

Clint shrugged as if unconcerned and said, "Sounds like even odds to me."

Hickok laughed and said, "You and I have to play poker, my friend."

"I hope we get the chance."

"That's enough talk," Ladd said. He made a motion to his men and they fanned out.

"I'll take the ones on the left; you take the right," Clint said.

"What about the one in the middle?"

"I've got ten dollars that says I work my way to him before you do."

Hickok laughed again and said, "You're on, my cocky friend."

Clint assumed that the other four men would key on Ladd, the man in the middle and the obvious leader. That put them at an immediate disadvantage, despite the odds. Four pairs of eyes would be on Ladd, and when he moved, they'd move.

Fortunately, by that time they'd most likely be dead.

Ladd moved first, as anticipated.

Clint ignored the two men on the right, leaving them to the man he'd heard called Hickok. He drew and quickly killed the two men on the left before either of them could draw. He turned his gun on Ladd and fired, striking the man once in the chest as his hand touched his gun. It was only then that he looked at the two men on the right, who were lying on the ground, dead.

He looked at Hickok, who was tucking one gun back into his belt. He had only bothered to draw one, leaving the other untouched.

"What about our bet?" Hickok asked.

"Let's take a look."

They walked to the bodies and turned their attention to the one in the middle, Ladd. He had two holes in his chest, no farther apart than the two spades on a deuce of spades.

"Well, that sure looks like a tie to me," Clint said to Hickok, holstering his gun.

"Agreed."

They checked each of the men in turn and found them all dead.

"Oh, James!" Jamie Tutt cried, coming abreast of them and grabbing Hickok's arm.

"Jamie, go home," Hickok told her, pulling his arm away from her and paying her little attention. Clint noticed at this point that she was a pretty thing, but now was not the time for her to be demanding Hickok's attention.

"James!"

"Go home!" he shouted.

She flinched as if he had struck her, then turned and fled, presumably in the direction of her home. Coming from that direction and passing her on the way was a tall man with a mustache who wore a badge and a stern look.

"We're going to have to talk to the marshal," Hickok said to Clint in a low tone, "but after that I'd be honored if you'd let me buy you a drink. Seems to me you may have saved my life today, friend."

Realizing that the man had only used one of the two guns available to him Clint said, "I'm not all that sure now that you needed me, but I'll gladly take that drink."

"Well, so much for that idea," Jim Courtwright said, moving away from the window.

"I'm going after Jamie," Tutt said, moving toward the door. "Find out who that other man is."

"All right," Courtwright said as Tutt went through the doors. He was curious about that, too.

"Excitement's over, folks," the stage driver said. "Let's get your bags down."

The stunning blonde, who had stepped down from the stagecoach only moments before, now let her eyes linger on James Butler Hickok. It had been some time since she had seen him, and he had, if anything, gotten better looking.

And the man who was with him was not bad, either.

She was glad she had made the trip.

Colonel George Ward Nichols barely heard the coach

driver's words. His eyes were also fixed on the well-dressed, man who was now speaking with the town marshal.

What luck! Only seconds off the coach and he had found his man! he thought.

# FOUR

After they finished talking with the marshal, who saw no reason to hold them, Clint and Hickok repaired to the Deadline Saloon for the drink Hickok had promised him. They had exchanged names in the marshal's office.

"You handle that gun pretty good," Hickok said to Clint.

"I noticed you only used one of yours," Clint said, "which is why I said that maybe I dealt myself in unnecessarily."

"The help was appreciated," Hickok said. "You took a big chance for someone you didn't even know. I'm in your debt."

They raised their glasses and drank to that debt.

"Do you know what that was all about?" Clint asked.

"I have a good idea," Hickok said. "The woman who was with me has a jealous brother."

"Jealous? Of his sister?"

"Dave Tutt served in the army with me and I know that at least once he and his friend, Jim Courtwright, betrayed me. We've been enemies ever since."

"And you're seeing his sister."

Hickok shrugged and said, "You've seen her."

"She's a pretty one, no doubt about that."

"I have a weakness for the pretty ones," Hickok admitted.

"That's apparently something else we have in common."

Hickok got up to buy a second round of drinks, just after Clint claimed that the third round would be on him.

When Hickok returned, Clint said, "I've heard of you, you know."

"Well, was any of it good?"

"Some," Clint said, and he then admitted, "some not so good. I've heard they call you Wild Bill, but the girl called you James. What should I call you?"

"Take your pick," Hickok said. "James Butler Hickok, Wild Bill, whatever you like. You've earned the right to call me whatever you want."

"I think I'll take Bill."

"Bill it is," Hickok said, and they drank to that.

"Clint, I'm sorry I can't say that I've heard of you," Hickok said. "The way you handle that gun, though, I'm surprised that I haven't."

"I keep a low profile."

"Keep handling that gun like that and it'll get higher."

"I'm fine the way I am, Bill. I've got no—"

"Wait a minute," Hickok interrupted, putting his drink down with a bang. "I have heard of you."

"Uh, really?"

"Haven't you been a lawman?"

"For a while, yeah."

"I've got it," Hickok said with satisfaction. "I read about you in the papers when I was in Fort Smith. Some reporter was calling you 'Gunsmith'."

"Yeah, I guess that's me," Clint replied uncomfortably.

In fact, there had been a very few write-ups about Clint Adams while he was a deputy sheriff, and one of the reporters had dubbed him Gunsmith, a name that stuck.

"You work on your own guns, right?"

"That's right."

"Sure, I've heard of you."

"I don't think too many people have, though."

"Like I said, that'll change. Damn, what a stroke of luck to run into you."

"Why is that?"

"I've got a piece that needs some work."

Clint laughed and said, "I'll be glad to take a look at it."

"Well, I'll drink to that," Hickok said, raising his glass. They drank to that and to a lot more.

"You see why I don't want you around Hickok?" Dave Tutt asked his sister. "That kind of thing could happen at any time. The man attracts trouble."

"That wasn't James's fault!"

"I don't care whose fault it was, I don't want you near him."

"You can't give me orders—" Jamie started to retort, but Tutt, tired of losing arguments to her, decided to try a new tact.

He slapped her across the face. Even though he did not hit her hard, the blow staggered her.

"That's enough, Jamie! Do you hear? I don't want to argue with you. Do you understand?"

"Oh, I understand, David," she said, looking at him with hatred in her eyes, "I understand only too well!"

When Colonel George Ward Nichols entered the Deadline Saloon, he was very pleased to see the man who had been identified to him as James Butler Hickok seated at a table there. He had done some background on the man, talking to some townspeople and the marshal, and now felt that it was time to approach the man himself.

He approached the table that Hickok was sharing with another man and introduced himself.

"Excuse me, my name is Colonel George Ward Nichols—"

"Colonel?" Hickok said, squinting up at the man. He

appeared to be more than a little drunk, which would not hurt Nichols's chances at all. "I ain't about to sign up for another hitch, Colonel."

"No, you don't understand, Mr. Hickok. I'm a writer and I'd like to talk to you."

Both Clint and Hickok inspected the man for a few moments. What they saw was a tall, thin man dressed in eastern finery, complete with a bowler hat and a cane. He appeared to be in his early fifties and the look in his eyes could only be described as hopeful.

"Well, sit down and start talking, Colonel," Hickok invited, "as long as you buy drinks while you talk."

"I'd be delighted to buy the drinks, Mr. Hickok, but I would prefer to do this alone," he said, looking at Clint and adding, "at least initially, if your friend doesn't mind."

"I don't mind," Clint said, "I've got to get some dinner anyway."

"I figured we could have dinner together," Hickok said to Clint.

"Well, tell me a good place and we'll meet there later, after your talk with Colonel Nichols."

"There's a café down the street, on the other side of the hotel. I'll meet you there in about an hour, if you can wait that long."

"I'll wait," Clint said. "See you then."

As Clint Adams left the saloon, Colonel Nichols said to Hickok, "Mr. Hickok, I want to make you famous."

Hickok squinted again and then said, "Well, keep talking."

# FIVE

When Hickok met Clint at the café, Clint was already flirting with the attractive waitress who had served him his coffee and who seemed to know Hickok.

"This jasper a friend of yours, Jim?"

"That he is, Clarice. You better treat him right if you know what's good for you."

"Honey," she said, giving them both a bold, bawdy wink, "I always know what's good for me. You gents give a holler when you're ready to order."

As Hickok sat down, Clint looked at him with unmasked admiration. He knew that Hickok must have been drinking with that Colonel Nichols for the better part of the past hour—and he had been drunk when Clint had left the saloon—but now the man showed little or no effects from all that whiskey and beer.

"You're gonna be very interested in this," Hickok told Clint.

"In what?"

"That fella, Colonel Nichols, he's come west to make somebody famous."

"How's he going to do that?"

"By writing about him," Hickok said, "by writing about him so that a bunch of easterners pay to read what he writes."

"And who's he going to write about?"

"Well, me, you ass," Hickok said, good-naturedly, "and you, too, if you play your cards right."

"Oh, no," Clint said, holding his hands up, "not me. What would he write about me, anyway?"

"What about that time you killed a dozen Indians single-handedly?"

"I never killed a dozen Indians, single-handed or otherwise."

Hickok smiled and said, "You have now."

"You lied?"

"Hell, it's one of the things I do best," Hickok said, "and I been doing it for the past hour. Why, I bet that writer fella filled up I don't know how many little notebooks with the things I told him—starting with what happened today."

"Bill, I don't know about this—"

"Now, originally he just wanted to write about me, even though he saw you there with me today." Looking properly humble, Hickok said. "He said I was flashier than you."

"What's he want me to do, grow my hair long?"

"That might not be a bad idea," Hickok said, "but I told him that if he writes about me he's gotta write about you, too, because we been friends for a long time."

"We just met today!"

"He don't have to know that," Hickok said slowly, as if speaking to a child. "Come on, Clint, haven't you ever told a lie before?"

"Once or twice, but never a whopper like the ones you must have told today."

"Well, I'll help you," Hickok assured him. "We'll practice until you're almost as good at it as I am."

"I don't want to practice," Clint said, "and I don't want to be written about. You can have it."

"We'll see," Hickok said, motioning to Clarice that they

were ready. "Let's have us a good dinner, and we'll talk about it more."

Hickok was wrong. *He* talked about it more while Clint split his time between listening and protesting—the latter to no avail.

Wild Bill Hickok was intent on making the Gunsmith famous in spite of himself!

"I told you I know what I want," Clarice said to Clint later on.

They were in his hotel room, in bed together, where Clint had had a feeling they would end up when they first saw each other.

The dinner he had shared with Hickok was a late one, and as they were finishing up, Clarice had been cleaning up to close. She had actually left the place at the same time they did—by design, Clint realized later.

"We'll talk tomorrow," Hickok had said to Clint after the Gunsmith had turned down his invitation to play a few hands of poker.

"Time enough for that tomorrow," Clint had replied. "I've got to get some rest."

Hickok looked from his new friend to Clarice, smiled, and said, "Sure."

As Hickok walked away, Clint had turned to Clarice and asked, "Where are you off to?"

"Where are you staying?"

"At the Springfield Hotel."

Linking her arm in his, she had said, "Then that's where I'm off to."

Clarice was in her twenties, although somewhat the worse for wear. She'd been a saloon girl or waitress most of her life, and it showed. Still, she had a full, firm body and enough enthusiasm to make up for any possible faults.

She was seated astride him now, his huge erection buried deep inside her. Her hands were behind her head and her back arched so that her large breasts were thrust forward. She was rotating her hips back and forth while Clint simply laid back eyeing her breasts, waiting for a chance to bring them down to his mouth. Finally he could wait no longer and he reached for her, pulling her down to him so he could suck her nipples.

She had offered to bathe first, but he had told her not to worry about it. Now he tasted the salt of her perspiration, and did not find it at all unpleasant.

"Mmmm," she moaned. As he continued to suck her nipples, she continued to ride his cock up and down until finally he felt her body begin to tremble. Reaching for her buttocks, he clamped his hands on them and allowed himself to ejaculate into her forcefully. Her orgasm overcame her and she began to moan and cry out as he held her tightly to him.

"Oh, God . . ." she said, rolling off him.

"Yeah," he agreed.

"Are you going to stay in town long?" she asked, letting her hand rest on his crotch, winding the hair there around her fingers.

"I don't know yet, Clarice."

"Have you known Hickok long?"

"Just met him today."

"Well," she said, "that makes two new friends you made in one day. Most people don't make that many in a year." There was a bitter edge to the statement that he chose to ignore. "Are you sleepy?" she asked.

"Yes. I rode a long way today."

"And I rode a long way just now," she said, smiling. "Do

you mind if I . . . stay the night?"

Still impressed by her boldness, Clint said, "Hell, no, I don't mind."

"Good," she said happily, making herself comfortable against him.

In moments the woman was asleep but, surprisingly, as tired as he was, Clint had trouble falling asleep himself. He kept thinking about the things Hickok had told him and, in spite of himself, he found the prospect of fame somewhat exciting.

He had no real way of knowing at the time that he was standing at a major crossroads in his life.

Wild Bill Hickok had a room in the Springfield House, the town's other hotel, and when he finally made his way back to it that night—finally feeling the effects of all of the whiskey he'd consumed, but somewhat richer for having found a poker game—he found someone waiting for him in his room.

Susannah Moore.

The blonde was gloriously naked and, as Hickok entered, she threw back the covers of the bed to reveal herself to him. He stared at her full, creamy-skinned breasts, her already taut, pink nipples, and her solid thighs.

"Susannah."

"It's been a long time, Jim."

It had, in fact, been three years and Hickok had never expected to see Susannah Moore again. Their earlier relationship had been somewhat imperfect, although the sexual part of it had never been a problem at all.

She was even lovelier than he remembered and, as he approached her and took her breasts in his hands, her hardened pink nipples scraped his palms. Her skin was as soft and smooth as he remembered, her breasts marvelously firm and full as he hefted them. Jamie Tutt was a lovely young woman, but Susannah Moore was something else again.

"What brings you here?" he asked.

"What does it matter?" she asked, reaching for him. "I'm here."

# SIX

During the next few days Hickok spent a lot of time with Colonel Nichols, much to the dismay of Ed Blaine, his campaign manager. It seemed to Blaine that Hickok was suddenly more concerned with becoming famous than he was with becoming marshal of Springfield—and the election was only weeks away.

Clint had become a confidant of Hickok to the extent that Blaine went to him with the problem. They had been introduced to each other on Clint's second day in town.

"This fella Nichols is taking up all Jim's time, Clint," Blaine complained, "and whatever he's not taking up, Susannah Moore is."

"Well, you can hardly blame him for the latter," Clint said. He, too, had been having some thoughts about Susannah Moore. If only she weren't Hickok's friend . . .

"Well, somebody's got to talk to him or he's going to lose this election."

"You want me to be that somebody?"

"He's got a lot of respect for you, Clint," Blaine pointed out. "He'll listen to you. Make him realize what he's giving up."

Clint deliberated a moment and then said, "All right, Ed, I'll talk to him, but he's having so much fun telling Nichols all those lies that I don't know if he'll listen."

"I appreciate your trying."

"I've got a suggestion for you, though," Clint said before Blaine could leave.

"What's that?"

"While I talk with Bill, you have a talk with Colonel Nichols. Between us maybe we can get something accomplished, eh?"

"Good idea."

Blaine stood up and left the Deadline Saloon and Clint walked to the bar and ordered another beer. He didn't know where Hickok was now—he could be with either Nichols or Susannah—but he knew that if he stayed put long enough Wild Bill would come walking in.

There was another problem that Clint wondered if Hickok knew about, and that was Jamie Tutt. Ever since Susannah had come to town, Hickok hadn't given Jamie a tumble. As pretty as Jamie was, she just couldn't match Susannah Moore's beauty.

By keeping his ears open, Clint had discovered that Jamie Tutt was now apparently angrier at Hickok than her brother Dave was. Dave Tutt was happy that Hickok was no longer seeing his sister.

Clint knew from experience that a woman could be as dangerous as any man when she was angry enough, and Jamie Tutt seemed angry enough.

Clint, meanwhile and in spite of his fantasies about Susannah Moore, had been keeping the waitress, Clarice Wells, very happy and vice versa. But the real reason that Clint had decided to stay in Springfield, however, was to see how the election came out, so he decided that maybe he did have a stake in changing Hickok's attitude.

As expected, Hickok finally showed up at the saloon with Colonel Nichols following and scribbling furiously into a notebook, just one of many such books he had filled while listening to Hickok's stories.

"And then what?" Nichols asked eagerly as they approached the bar.

"And then I had a drink, which is what I'm gonna to do right now."

Nichols shook his head in open admiration.

"He kills five men with four bullets without blinking an eye and then has a drink," he said aloud.

"Ah, there's my friend and partner, Clint Adams," Hickok said, carrying his drink to Clint's table.

As Nichols approached the table also, Clint said, "Excuse me, Colonel, why don't you go over to the hotel and write all that out while I have a talk with Wild Bill, here."

"Good idea, lad, good idea," Nichols said. "I want to get this into good prose while it's fresh in my mind. I'll be talking to you later, Wild Bill."

"That's for sure, Colonel, that's for sure," Hickok said, sitting down with Clint. "And don't forget about my friend Clint, you hear?"

"No, sir, I won't forget," Nichols said and scurried out of the saloon, headed for his hotel where Ed Blaine was waiting for him, Clint hoped.

"How can you stand that weasel?" Clint asked.

"Hey, he's making me famous and paying for the privilege."

"Paying?"

"Sure. Do you realize how much money that jasper is gonna make off these stories? All I did was ask for a little advance and he came across."

"Bill, we have to talk."

"About what?"

"About the election," Clint said. "Ed's more than a little worried."

"The election?" Hickok said. "Hell, that's Ed's job—"

"I don't think Ed Blaine sees it that way, Bill," Clint said, interrupting him, "and if you want the truth, I don't, either."

"What are you talking about?"

"Ed can't win an election with a candidate who doesn't give a damn."

"Who doesn't give a damn—" Hickok began to bluster, but Clint cut him short again.

"All you care about is becoming a legend in some overblown dude's newspaper."

"If I didn't know better, Clint," Hickok said, frowning, "I'd think you were jealous."

Clint stiffened and stood up. "I guess you don't know me at all, Bill," Clint said, pushing back his chair to leave.

"Okay, okay, wait a minute," Hickok said, putting his hand out for Clint to stay. "Sit back down, will you? Don't be so sensitive; I didn't mean it."

Clint hesitated a moment and then sat back down.

"Maybe you're right," Hickok said, "maybe I am paying too much attention to the Colonel—"

"And Susannah Moore?"

Hickok paused, then said, "And Susannah, although you can't really blame me for that."

"No, I don't," Clint agreed, "but I'd certainly put the Colonel aside for a shot at the election, Bill, wouldn't you?"

"Yeah," Hickok said, "yeah, I guess you're right. Look, I'll go and find Ed and we can get started on a real campaign. Maybe we can still pull this thing out."

"I think you've got a good shot, if you concentrate on it."

"And I will," Hickok said, standing up, and then he added, "I can always talk to the Colonel at night."

Clint watched Hickok leave the saloon and shook his head. Well, maybe the man could become a legend and a marshal.

*     *     *

Blaine was indeed waiting for Nichols in the lobby of the hotel and approached the man as he entered.

"Colonel?"

"Yes?"

"I'm Ed Blaine," Blaine said. "I'm managing Hickok's campaign for marshal."

"Oh, yes. I've seen you."

"I'd like to talk to you."

"About what?"

"Hickok."

"Well, I've got some notes to transcribe," Nichols said impatiently.

"It'll only take a moment," Blaine said. "We can talk right here."

"All right. What's on your mind?"

"Like I said, I'm handling Jim's campaign for town marshal."

"So?"

"So it hasn't been much of a campaign since you came to town."

"You're blaming me?"

"I am. You're filling his head with nonsense. You and I are older than he is, Nichols; we know that the promise of fame can turn a young man's mind away from the more important things in life."

"Like being the marshal of a one-horse town?"

"It's a start."

Nichols frowned and said, "Your name is familiar to me. Were you a writer?"

Blaine made note of the fact that Nichols took special delight in using the word *were*.

"I was—for a while."

"I see."

"You see what?"

"Well, I'm a successful writer, Mr. Blaine. Maybe you're more concerned with your own jealousy than with Mr. Hickok's campaign?"

"I'm going to forget you said that, Nichols," Blaine said, deliberately dropping the man's title, "this time. "Just keep in mind that if Jim Hickok loses this election because of you, I'm going to take it personally."

They made a comical sight, these two portly scribes who would be more accustomed to handling pens than any kind of weapon, as they stood in the hotel lobby glaring at each other belligerently.

"Is that a threat?"

"A promise," Blaine said, and then turning to leave he added, "and if you like I'll put it in writing."

Hickok had been gone only few moments when the doors swung open and Jamie Tutt walked in. She took a quick look around the room, which was nearly empty, and then zeroed in on Clint, whom she recognized as Wild Bill Hickok's new friend.

"Someone said that James was here," she said, making it sound like an accusation. She was wearing shirt and pants which fit her well and showed off a trim, shapely figure. She really was a pretty little thing and, given time, she would probably be able to give Susannah Moore some competition. Unfortunately, she was impatient.

"He was here," Clint said. "You just missed him."

"Where did he go," she demanded, "to be with that blond bitch?"

"I believe he went to see Ed Blaine about his campaign for marshal."

"Ha!" she said. "All of a sudden he's worried about the election?"

"I guess so."

The bartender came over and said, "Excuse me, Jamie, but you shouldn't be in here."

"Don't tell me where I should be!"

The bartender tossed Clint a pleading glance and Clint nodded imperceptibly. "Come on, Miss Tutt," Clint said, standing up, "I'll walk you out."

He took hold of her arm gently and that seemed to set her off. "Take your hands off me!" she shouted. She attempted to slap him, but he was too quick for her, catching her arm in his hand.

"Jamie—" he began, but he was cut off by the appearance of two men.

Dave Tutt and Jim Courtwright passed through the doors, and the first thing Tutt saw was Clint Adams holding his sister's arm.

"Get your hands off her, Adams," he said. He, too, recognized Clint as Hickok's new friend and was incensed to see his sister being treated that way.

"Take it easy, Tutt," Clint began, "I was just trying to—"

Dave Tutt did not give him a chance to finish. He charged Clint, and Clint released Jamie's arm and pushed her aside so that he could face Tutt. The man had no intention of letting him explain, and he had no intention of accepting a beating from the larger man.

The big man balled his fists and swung a right at Clint, a wild roundhouse blow that, had it landed, might have taken his head off. Instead, the Gunsmith ducked beneath the blow and pounded one of his own into Tutt's belly. The big man grunted and staggered, due more to his lack of balance than to the effect of the blow.

Regaining his balance, Dave Tutt looked as if he wanted to

go for his gun. Clint tensed, ready to draw his own gun if necessary, when they were both frozen by the sound of the bartender's voice.

"Hold it!" the man shouted.

Both Tutt and Clint looked at the man who was standing behind the bar with a shotgun aimed their way.

"You fellas want to kill each other, that's fine, but take it outside my place."

Tutt made a move toward Clint, ignoring the bartender. "Tutt," he shouted, cocking the shotgun, "I asked your sister to leave because she's a young lady, but I'm telling you, get out of here before I pull this trigger."

Tutt turned his murderous gaze from the bartender back to Clint. "Adams was only trying to get her to leave quietly," the bartender tried to explain. "This ain't no kind of place for her."

Courtwright, who was standing behind Tutt, said, "Come on, Dave, let's take Jamie out of here."

Tutt did not react for a moment, and then he said to Clint, "Another time, Adams."

Clint simply shrugged unconcernedly and said, "Up to you."

Tutt looked at his sister angrily and said, "Let's go, Jamie!"

"I'm going," she said, just as angry as he, "but not with you," and with that she stormed out. Tutt backed up to the door and, after Courtwright had gone out, backed out after him, throwing a last malevolent look at Clint.

Clint looked at the bartender and asked, "Want me to leave?"

"Hell, no," the bartender said, putting down his shotgun. "Want another drink?"

# SEVEN

After one more drink, Clint decided that he had spent enough time in the Deadline Saloon. Indeed, he had spent most of his time there since arriving in town, and only after the incident with Dave Tutt did he find out that the bartender's name was Joe Brewer.

"See you later, Joe."

Brewer waved and then began to serve some of the men who had just entered. It was about time for the place to fill up, but Clint wanted some air.

Outside the daylight was starting to fade, and as Clint stepped off the walk to cross the street, he saw Susannah Moore walking toward him.

"If you're looking for Hickok, he's not in here."

Looking amused, she said, "I'm not looking for Jim; I'm looking for you."

"Me? Why?"

"I've been in town a few days and I know you and Jim are friends. I'd like us to become friends, too."

"Why?"

"Take me to dinner and we'll discuss why."

Clint looked at her and found her possibly one of the most beautiful women he'd ever seen. Her breasts thrust upward proudly from the bodice of her dress. Round and firm they were, and looking at them made his hands itch.

Could he trust himself with her? She was, after all, Hickok's woman—that is, as far as he knew.

"I won't bite you," she promised.

"All right," Clint said, "dinner it is. There's a café just down the block."

"Fine. Lead the way."

When they were settled at a table, Clint realized that he'd made a mistake. Without thinking, he'd taken Susannah to the café where Clarice worked, and he realized his error when Clarice slammed down his plate. Susannah's plate was put down with somewhat less force. Then Clarice stalked away.

"A friend of yours?" Susannah asked, looking amused.

"I think she was," Clint said regretfully.

"I'm sorry."

"Forget it."

"I understand you saved Jim's life your first day here."

"You should know," Clint said. "It was your first day as well, and you saw it."

It was disconcerting to be seated across from a lovely woman he felt he couldn't touch. Her face was narrow and had high cheekbones, and the structure seemed to enhance the effect of her big, startlingly blue eyes.

"Yes, I did," she said. "I was just trying to make conversation."

"If we have to force conversation, maybe we shouldn't be here," he said.

"Oh, I don't think so," she said, touching his hand with one of hers. "I think we're having trouble because we know we're attracted to one another."

"What?"

"I'd like you to take me to bed, Clint."

His heart began to race and he became annoyed with himself—and with her—because of it.

"I can't do that, Susannah."

"You don't want to?" she asked, looking faintly surprised. "You don't find me attractive."

"Don't play games," he said. "You know how beautiful you are and that any man would want you."

"Then what's the problem?"

"You know that, too."

"Jim?"

"Yes. He's my friend."

"Friends share, don't they?"

"Not women, they don't."

"Clint, you don't think that Jim and I are in love or anything, do you?"

"I don't know."

"Well, let me tell you that we're not. God, we could never be in love. Out of bed I don't think we can even stand one another."

"That may be, Susannah, but—"

"Damn it, Clint Adams," she said, "I want you, and I know you want me. I've seen you looking at me."

"I won't deny that."

"Well, Clint Adams," she said, sitting back in her chair, "go find your friend and ask him; he'll tell you it's all right."

"Susannah—"

"All right," she said abruptly, "eat your dinner, then, but remember that I came to you and offered myself to you. Your loyalty to your friend is admirable but misguided in this case, I assure you."

For a moment Clint was tempted to go and find Hickok and put the question to him, but he dispelled that thought with a slight shake of his head. "Let's eat."

"Yes," she said, seeming annoyed with him now, "let's."

Following dinner, they split up with few words exchanged. He went back to his hotel and she went back to hers—the only other hotel in town. He was annoyed at himself over the missed opportunity. What would it have hurt to take her to his bed. After all, she had asked for it, and she was damned beautiful.

Had it been an act of strength, of loyalty to his friend? Or was it, as she said, misguided loyalty?

Maybe he'd never know, but he knew one thing: Having dinner with her at that café had certainly ruined his chances of any further pleasures with Clarice.

Having committed himself to staying until after the election, he was starting to wish that maybe Hickok would withdraw and go after his fame with Colonel Nichols.

It was starting to look like a lonely two weeks ahead.

# EIGHT

When Clint went back to his room at the Springfield Hotel, there was someone there waiting for him. This was not an unusual occurrence in the life of the Gunsmith. It had happened before, and he knew from experience that it was either a woman or someone who wanted to blow his head off.

This time it was a woman. He could smell her as he opened the door.

Was it Clarice?

"Hello."

It wasn't Clarice. It was Jamie Tutt—in bed with the sheet pulled up to her neck. "Hello," she said.

"Jamie?"

"You remember," she said, batting her eyelashes at him. "I'm flattered."

He recognized that she was attempting to be both alluring and sophisticated, but she was too inexperienced to pull it off successfully.

Still, she was very pretty.

"Jamie, this is a mistake," he said to her.

"No," she said, shaking her head, "it's not."

"If I let you stay, it is," he said, but he already knew that he was going to let her stay, that he was going to make a mistake. He was too stirred by Susannah, and Clarice wasn't about to show up.

"Tell me you don't like me," she challenged.

47

"Are you undressed under there?" he asked.

She took her arms out from beneath the sheet and put them at her sides, tightening the sheet around her. It molded itself to her to the point that he could see the outline of her nipples, which were erect.

"Can't you tell?"

He walked to the bed and put his hand over one of her breasts, feeling its firmness through the sheet.

He thumbed a nipple through the sheet and said, "Yeah, I can tell, Jamie."

She didn't make it easy. Her body was young and firm, but she didn't know enough to keep quiet and enjoy it. Instead, she talked constantly, and while she talked, the bitterness came out.

As he was sucking on a nipple, she said, "I'll bet you wish you were with Susannah Moore."

"Hmmm?" he said, picking his head up so he could frown at her.

"She's out to here," she said, holding her hands out over her breasts, "like a cow. Men like women like that. Cows, I mean."

"Men," he said firmly, "like woman who moan and groan during sex and don't talk. Jamie, believe me when I say that you've got beautiful breasts, and if you'll keep quiet, maybe we can enjoy each other."

She made a face at him and he decided to simply get it over with. He was throbbing with an insatiable need for Susannah Moore, and drawing this coupling out wasn't going to help relieve it.

He climbed on top of her and pierced her so savagely that her breath caught in her throat and stuck there. He started driving in and out of her, holding her slim, tight buttocks in his hands. It was a position he favored because it gave him control over the tempo—although there wasn't much tempo to control in this instance, just a wild, uncontrolled slamming of flesh on flesh as he pumped himself in and out of her faster and faster. He was plain and simply seeking his own release with no regard for her pleasure.

Jamie's arms and legs wrapped around him tightly as she simply held on for dear life. The only sounds that came out of her mouth thereafter were the moans and groans he had previously mentioned.

He thought of Susannah Moore the whole time and felt slight guilt.

He watched Jamie as she dressed, and he was sure that she was sorry she had come. She had done it to spite Hickok, and maybe to spite her brother, and now she was regretting it.

So was Clint.

Dressed, she stood up straight and faced him. He could have predicted what she said next. "I'll bet you were thinking of Susannah Moore the whole time."

"You're right," he answered honestly, and she stormed out.

To hell with her. His need taken care of—but his desire still present—he fell into a fitful sleep filled with dreams of an out of reach Susannah Moore, a jealous Clarice, and a bitter Jamie.

# NINE

In the morning he had breakfast in the hotel dining room and met Ed Blaine there.

"Mind if I join you?" Blaine inquired.

"Have a seat."

Blaine sat down and gave his order to the waiter who brought Clint's breakfast.

"Coffee and biscuits," he said.

"That's all?" Clint asked, preparing to attack his steak and eggs.

"I'm trying to lose weight."

Never having had that problem, Clint did not comment.

"I want to thank you," Blaine said.

"For what?"

"For talking to Jim. Whatever you said, it worked—for a while, anyway. You and he are the same age, aren't you?"

"I guess."

"I wish he was as levelheaded as you are."

"You'll make me blush," Clint said. "Did you talk to the Colonel?"

"We growled at each other," Blaine said. "He thinks I'm jealous of his success as a writer."

"Are you?"

"I've yet to see it."

"Why don't you see if you can run the Colonel out of town?" Clint suggested.

51

"That's not my style. If I tried to pick up a gun I'd probably shoot myself in the foot."

"I'm sure he'd have the same problem," Clint said. "Maybe you can outwrite him."

"If I could do that," Blaine said, "I'd still be a news-paperman."

Clint liked Blaine even more because there wasn't a trace of bitterness in his tone when he said that.

The waiter came and Clint said, "Eat your breakfast."

They were working on a second pot of coffee when Clint asked, "Where is Bill now?"

Blaine shrugged. "Sleeping, talking to the Colonel, plowing Susannah's field—I don't know. As long as he meets me at the town hall in an hour, I don't care what he's doing now. He's got to tell the town biddies how he'll keep Springfield safe when he's elected marshal."

"He should tell them he'll shoot it up if he's not elected marshal."

Blaine stared at him a moment and then said, "You know, that might just work."

"Tell me about Bill and Susannah?" Clint asked.

"What is there to tell?"

"Did you know her before?"

"Not before she came here. I didn't even know Bill before he came here."

"How did you end up managing his campaign."

"Well, let's face it," Blaine said, "he certainly couldn't manage it himself."

"Is Susannah anything more than a distraction to him?"

"She appeals to you, huh?" Blaine said. "Well, why not? She appeals to me, too."

"Yeah, but did she ask you to take her to bed?"

Blaine's mouth fell open and he said, "She asked you?"

Clint nodded.

"No woman's ever asked me," Blaine said wistfully. He looked at Clint and asked with great interest, "What did you say?"

"No."

"Wow."

"I know," Clint said, shaking his head, "I still can't believe it myself."

"Because of Hickok?"

Clint nodded again. "She's his woman, isn't she?"

"Well, I don't think he's in love with her, if that's what you mean," Blaine said, "and I don't know how territorial he is about her. If you're interested, why don't you just ask him?"

"The opportunity is gone," Clint said, as if mourning the passing of a dear friend.

"Maybe not. Women like Susannah, they're not satisfied with one man."

"Maybe there's hope for you yet," Clint said teasingly.

Blaine looked thoughtful for a moment—his mind no doubt conjuring up the image of Susannah begging him to take her to bed. "Would you believe I think I'd turn her down, too?" he asked.

Clint pondered that for a moment and then said, "No."


"I don't care what you say," Tutt said to Jim Courtwright. "She came in late last night and I know she was with Hickok."

"Hickok's paying too much attention to Susannah Moore to be with Jamie, Dave," Courtwright said, and then with a dreamy look on his face, he added, "Not that I can blame him. That one is a real beauty."

They were having breakfast in the café, being waited on by a rather glum Clarice.

"And what's wrong with my sister?" Tutt asked, glowering belligerently.

"Nothing, Dave," Courtwright said hurriedly, "nothing at all."

Mollified, Tutt went on, "Well, I've had it with Wild Bill Hickok. I'm sending out a message today that will solve my problem —our problem—once and or all."

Unsure he wanted to hear the answer—and unsure they were talking about a common problem anymore— Courtwright asked, "To who?"

"To somebody who can help with this problem. In fact, two men."

Courtwright leaned forward with a worried frown and asked, "Who are we talking about, Dave?"

"The Turner brothers."

"The Turner brother?" Courtwright said in surprise.

Tutt nodded and said, "Elmo and Ethan Turner."

Courtwright knew who the Turner brothers were. They were two of the meanest killers.

"But they're uncontrollable!"

"They're not so bad," Tutt said unconvincingly. "Besides, I've known them for a long time. They'll do this for me."

Courtwright didn't have to ask Tutt what he meant by that.

"You tried that already, Dave, and ended up getting five trail bums killed."

"The Turner brothers aren't trail bums, Jim. They're bona fide gunmen."

"And crazy."

"I can handle them."

"If you're not careful, they'll do what you pay them to do, and then take this town apart for fun."

"As long as Hickok ends up dead," Tutt said with feeling, "the Turners can have a little fun afterward."

# TEN

Clint decided to mosey over to the town hall and watch Hickok address the town biddies, as Ed Blaine called them. Actually, they were the Women for a Peaceful Springfield, and they carried a lot of weight with their voting husbands.

To Clint's surprise, Hickok was smooth, charming, and well spoken, and he could tell that most of the women had been won over by his manner. He told both Hickok and Ed Blaine as much afterward.

"Well, I'm glad to hear that," Blaine said. "I'm just starting to think that maybe we have a chance in this election after all."

"I always knew I had a chance, Ed," Hickok said, slapping his campaign manager on the back, "and it got better as soon as I hired you."

Blaine looked at Hickok and said, "As long as you realize that if you do become town marshal, it will be entirely due to my brilliance as manager."

"Not only will I realize it," Hickok said, playfully poking his friend in the chest with a stiff forefinger, "but I'll pin a deputy's badge on your chest. Now, what do you think of that?"

Blaine held up his hands and said gravely, "That won't be necessary."

He excused himself then and said that he had another meeting to set up.

"He's a hard worker," Clint commented as he and Hickok left the hall.

"That he is," Hickok said. "I'm glad you made me realize I was making a mistake. He hired on in good faith, and I want to show him that he's not wasting his time."

"Between the two of you," Clint said, "I think you can pull it off. From what I've seen while I've been here, the present marshal is pretty much invisible."

"He's been in the job for a while, though," Blaine said. "That usually counts for something."

"What about you?" Hickok asked.

"What about me?" Clint asked, wondering what he was talking about.

"How would you feel about putting on a deputy marshal's badge?"

Clint rubbed his jaw and gave the offer some thought. When the war came, he had been wearing a badge, and he gave it up to enlist. Maybe it was time to pick it up again.

"Why don't we wait until after the election and then we can discuss it."

"All right," Hickok said, "but think it over in the meantime."

"How many deputys are you going to need?"

"One or two, I suppose," Hickok said. "Springfield's pretty tame, actually, compared to some of the other places I've been." He shrugged his shoulders and said, "What could happen here?"

"As long as your friend Tutt is around to hire men to come after you, a lot."

"Too bad we can't prove he did hire them," Hickok said. "Might get him out of my hair for a while."

"I had a run-in with him myself yesterday," Clint said and then went on to describe the incident.

"I guess I haven't been real fair to Jamie, huh?"

"Maybe not."

"It's just that I haven't seen Susannah in such a long time."

"What's to that, anyway?" Clint asked, even before he realized he was going to.

Hickok shrugged and said, "Not much, I guess. We enjoy each other, but I'm not all that sure we like each other."

"Sounds like an odd relationship."

"It could hardly be called a relationship," Hickok said. "Truth of the matter is, I don't think she's a one-man woman and I know I'm not a one-woman man."

"You mean you wouldn't mind if she . . . slept with somebody else?"

Hickok grinned at Clint and said, "Not as long as he was a friend. You been thinking about it?"

"The thought has crossed my mind once . . . a dozen times."

"Can't blame you for that," Hickok said. "Take your best shot."

Clint didn't bother telling Hickok that he had already passed up his best shot and didn't anticipate another coming along in the near future.

# ELEVEN

The Turner brothers were in Caldwell, Missouri, not far from Springfield, when Dave Tutt's message caught up to them.

"Lookee here, El," Ethan Turner said, showing Elmo the piece of paper.

"Now, you know I can't read, Ethan," Elmo complained. "What for you always doing that to me?"

"Forgot."

Ethan, the younger brother, read the message to Elmo, who was almost a full minute older than his brother. They were identical twins, both tall and skinny with long necks and big hands.

"Sounds like Dave Tutt got himself a real problem there," Elmo said after he'd heard the message. "He don't say who the jasper is who's givin' him so much trouble?"

Ethan frowned at the message, moving his lips as he read it again, and then said, "Nope. He does say that he'll pay us a hundred dollars each, though."

Elmo scratched at his head vigorously. "Hundred ain't such a much," he opined.

"How much we got now between us?"

Elmo thought that one over a moment and then said, "Two dollars, I reckon." The two brothers exchanged looks and then Elmo said, "Hundred's better than nothin'."

"Besides," his brother added, taking out his .45 and cradling it in a hand, "we ain't killed nobody in at least a week."

Susannah Moore was bored, and there were several reasons for that. One was Wild Bill Hickok's sudden commitment to his campaign for town marshal. The second reason was that when he wasn't campaigning, Hickok was in a saloon till all hours, telling lies to Colonel Nichols. The third reason was that Clint Adams had turned down her offer to go to bed. This was also a cause for concern for the beauteous Susannah because she could count on the fingers of one hand the number of men who had turned her down before. She was also annoyed because she had actually had a yen for Clint Adams and still did, only she wasn't so sure she wanted to chance being turned down again.

So, instead of approaching Clint Adams again, Susannah decided to take a turn around town and see if there weren't any other interesting men to be seen—and had.

That was when she saw Dave Tutt.

Tutt and Courtwright were standing by the livery stable, for Courtwright had wanted to check on his horse.

"Isn't that Hickok's new woman?" he asked Tutt.

Tutt looked over at her and said, "She ain't so new, the way I hear. They knew each other before, but yeah, that's her, all right. Couldn't very well mistake her for anyone else, not the way she looks."

"Looks like she sees something over here that might interest her," Courtwright commented.

"Well, it sure as hell couldn't be you," Tutt said, "but why don't I go over and ask her so we can be sure."

"Dave," Courtwright said, "that's Hickok's woman."

"So?" Tutt asked. "It didn't bother him to bed my sister, did it?"

"You don't know—"

"Like hell I don't," Tutt said, yanking his arm out of his friend's grip. "I'll see you later."

Courtwright watched nervously as Tutt crossed the street and approached Susannah Moore, whose face lit up in a smile that put the sun to shame.

He hoped his friend wouldn't end up getting burned.

Clint Adams, on the way to the livery stable himself to give his horse, Jake, some exercise, stopped short when he saw Susannah Moore and Dave Tutt deep in conversations—what was a very flirtatious conversation.

Apparently, Susannah Moore was not all that particular about whom she offered herself to—which didn't make Clint Adams feel very flattered.

He faded into a shop's doorway and watched for a while until Susannah finally linked her arm in Dave Tutt's and they began to walk his way. Hastily, he opened the door of the shop and entered, then moved toward the window. Susannah and Tutt went by, and as he was about to leave the store, an older woman came up behind him and asked in an amused tone, "Can I help you with something?"

He turned and said, "Oh, I'm sorry." He looked around for the first time and became aware of the kind of store he had entered. It was a dress shop. "I'm sorry," he said again. "Wrong store."

As he made for the door, his face burning, she called out, "Come back if you change your mind."

Outside, he looked down the street and saw Susannah and Dave Tutt walking in the direction of her hotel, Springfield House.

Remembering what Hickok had said about not minding

whom she slept with as long as it was a friend, he fervently hoped that they wouldn't run into Wild Bill in the hotel lobby.

He entertained the thought of following them farther, but decided against it. They were two adults and what they did was their own business.

He continued on to the livery and entered with intentions of saddling Jake and taking him for a ride. As he entered, he saw Jim Courtwright examining his horse's hindquarters. The man looked up when he heard Clint approaching, and as their eyes locked, Courtwright stood up straight.

"I don't want any trouble, Adams."

"I'm not here looking for trouble . . . Courtwright, is it?"

"That's right."

"I'm just here to look after my horse."

"Me, too." Courtwright's eyes flicked nervously toward the door and Clint could tell what he was thinking.

"Yeah, I saw your friend outside."

"What are you gonna do?"

"About what?"

"He was with Hickok's woman," Courtwright said, "and Hickok's your friend, ain't he?"

"Tutt's your friend, isn't he?"

"Yeah, so?"

"What are you going to do?"

"Nothing."

"Why?"

"It's none of my business."

"That's a good attitude," Clint said. "That's exactly the way I feel." Courtwright hesitated and Clint said, "Look, Courtwright, all I came to do was saddle my horse and give him some exercise. Why don't you just go ahead and do what you were doing?"

"Okay."

Clint moved toward Jake's stall and began to saddle him. He was aware that Courtwright was watching him warily. When the horse was saddled, he mounted and rose past Courtwright. He stopped at the door and turned in his saddle to find the man still watchimg him carefully. "What's your interest in this, Courtwright?"

"In what?"

"In whatever feud Dave Tutt and Hickok have going."

"It's not just between them," Courtwright said. "It's with me, too."

"Comc on, Courtwright—"

"And it's Hickok's doing. He's got some crazy idea that Dave and me betrayed him during the war. He holds a hell of a grudge, Wild Bill Hickok does."

"Did you betray him?"

Courtwright hesitated a moment and then said, "That doesn't matter, Adams. As long as Hickok thinks we did, he won't lct up on us. He'll keep at us until—"

"Until?"

"Forget it," Courtwright said. "It's none of your business."

"You're right about that, Courtwright," Clint agreed. "See you around."

"Sure."

As Clint cleared the doors and left the livery, both men started breathing a little easier.

The Gunsmith knew that wouldn't last long.

# TWELVE

Jim Courtwright was waiting for Dave Tutt when he came out of her hotel. "You're crazy," Courtwright said to his friend. He pushed off the wall he was leaning against and flicked his cigarette into the street.

"You wouldn't say that if you'd been through what I just been through," Tutt said, smiling. "That's a real woman, Jim, believe me."

"She's also Hickok's woman and Adams saw the two of you together. If he tells Hickok—"

"Will he?"

"He's says not."

"Well, if he does, I guess Wild Bill will come after me, huh?"

"Probably."

"The Turners should be here soon," Tutt said, "and that would give them just the excuse they need. This may work out, Jim. Don't worry about it."

"Yeah, sure," Courtwright said nervously. "You gonna see her again?" he asked, jerking his head toward her hotel.

Tutt got a dreamy look on his face then and said, "God, I hope so."

Upstairs, an unfulfilled Susannah Moore vowed never to see Tutt again or any other muscle-bound man. He'd flexed and preened before her as he undressed and then proceeded to pursue his own pleasures while totally ignoring hers. He came with a great roar and then climbed off her, dressed, and left like he'd just given her the best roll of her life.

Not even close.

Clint Adams wouldn't be that way—she just knew he wouldn't.

She decided to give Clint Adams another chance, and she hoped he'd make the most of it.


An hour later when Clint returned to the stable from exercising Jake, there was no sign of Courtwright and his horse was in its stall. Clint took a look at the horse and found that he had a bad stone bruise on the hoof of his right foreleg. The horse wouldn't be going anywhere for a while. The man had had a legitimate reason for being in the stable.

Leaving the livery, he decided to go to the Deadline for a drink and a game of poker. The drink was a cold beer, but the poker game was no bargain. Clint knew all of the players. Two of them were tradesmen from town; the third man was easily recognizable due to his girth and the bowler hat on the table at his elbow. It was Colonel Nichols.

"Mind if I sit in, fellas?" Clint asked, approaching the table.

Two of the men looked up at him.

"There's an empty chair," one of them said unconcernedly. "One man's money is as good as the next's." Judging from the money in front of Nichols, maybe they were hoping that new blood would change their luck.

Nichols was intent on shuffling the cards and did not look at the new player until he was ready to deal. "Ah, Mr. Adams."

"Colonel Nichols."

"Have you seen our mutual friend, Mr. Hickok?"

"He's probably out campaigning."

"Ah, yes," Nichols said, dealing out five cards to each man, "he has become rather intent on winning that election. Must be something that Blaine fella said to him, hmmm?"

"That's as it should be," Clint said, picking up his cards. "He should be worried about the election and not about telling you stories."

"Now you sound like Blaine. I didn't come to this town to report on some local election." Suddenly Nichols looked at him sharply and asked, "And what about you? Do you have any stories to tell?"

Clint said, "I have a decent hand here, and I open for five dollars."

The other two men called, and Nichols called and raised five.

Clint studied the man for a moment and Nichols said, "You westerners do not have a monopoly on poker, Mr. Adams. Back home, I'm considered quite good."

"I guess it's lucky for me we're not there," Clint said. "I call."

"Cards, gentlemen?"

Clint drew two, the other two men drew one and three respectively, while the Colonel took one.

"All right, gentlemen," Colonel Nichols said, "let's go around the table." Suddenly the Colonel did not look like the comical character Clint had.

"I'll bet ten," Clint said.

The other two players folded, leaving the play up to the Colonel.

"Well, I can't let you just walk off with it, can I?" the man asked. "I'll see your ten and raise you twenty."

No, Clint thought, don't let me walk away with it if you can steal it.

Clint's cards were flat on the table and he didn't look at them again. He didn't have to. He knew what they were and looking at them wouldn't change them.

"I'll call your twenty and raise twenty."

"Mr. Hickok tells me that you have quite a reputation yourself, Mr. Adams, one that almost rivals his own. He says they call you the Gunsmith."

"Right now," Clint said, giving Nichols a level look, "I'd just like you to call me."

Nichols returned Clint's stare, his eyes turning hard in his pudgy face. "Yes," he said, "I'll be you would." He threw his cards in and added, "The deal passes to you."

When Hickok walked into the saloon with Ed Blaine, they spotted Clint Adams and Colonel Nichols playing poker, head to head. There was no one else at the table.

"Ed, get two beers, will you?"

"Sure, Jim."

Hickok walked over to watch the two men play. From the way the money was divided on the table, he could tell that Clint was winning big. He figured that there probably had been other players in the game at one time, but it had come down to these two.

Blaine came over and handed Hickok a beer, and the two men watched the game in silence, standing so that they couldn't see either man's hand.

"This is the last hand, Colonel," Clint said, dealing out the cards.

"That's not for the winner to say," Nichols said. "Back home we give losers a chance to get their money back."

"If everybody did that," Clint said, completing the deal, "there'd never be any winner or loser, Colonel. Everybody would break even. That's not why they call it gambling. Not out here anyway."

Nichols looked at Hickok as if asking for help, but Wild

Bill just sipped his beer. Blaine averted his eyes, just in case the Colonel looked to him, as well.

"All right," the Colonel said, picking up his cards.

"Your bet, Colonel."

The Colonel looked at his hand and, although he had three of a kind, more than enough to open with, his eyes turned crafty, and he decided to check and let Clint open; that way he could raise immediately. His plan was to get as much of his money back on this last hand as he could.

But his plan didn't work. "I check," he said.

"I fold," Clint said, dropping his cards on the table and standing up.

"What?" the Colonel said. "But you can't!"

"Why not?"

"I have—I thought—" the Colonel said. He got to his feet quickly, dropping his hand face up on the table where everybody could get a good look at the cards.

"Three queens," Ed Blaine said in disbelief.

"Is that the way they play poker in the east, Colonel?" Clint asked.

"Looks like the game's over," Hickok said. "Can I buy you two boys a drink?"

"Sure," Clint said.

"Was he trying to pump you for stories, Clint?" Hickok asked.

"I'm not a storyteller, Bill," Clint said, "you know that. The Colonel got nothing out of me."

"You're wrong," Nichols said then, backing away from the table. "I learned a lot about you today, Adams, just from the way you play cards." With that the Colonel turned and left the saloon.

"What was that all about?" Hickok asked, as he, Blaine, and Clint walked to the bar to get Clint a beer.

"Your Colonel may not be all that he appears to be," Clint explained.

"Why do you say that?"

"He was right about one thing," Clint said, accepting a beer from Blaine. "You do learn a lot from sitting across a poker table from a man."

"What'd you learn about Nichols?" Ed Blaine asked, hoping that it would be something that would convince Hickok to have nothing further to do with the man.

"I'm not sure, Ed," Clint said honestly, "but I do think there's more to that funny, little man than meets the eye—and it may not be so funny."

"What do you think he meant when he said he learned something about you?" Hickok asked.

Clint shrugged and said, "I guess he learned a little about how we play poker here in the west."

# THIRTEEN

Returning to his room for the night, Clint more than half hoped that he'd find somebody in his room again—someone like Susannah Moore, although he would have settled for Clarice Wells.

He entered the room; there was no one there.

While undressing and hanging his gunbelt on the bedpost, he was acutely aware of a fire burning inside of him, one that had been started by Susannah Moore. He sat on the bed, annoyed at the erection that was raging inside his longjohns.

Susannah Moore. He couldn't stop thinking about her, and even if he was able to stop himself consciously, his hard, twitching erection wouldn't let him.

Hell, even if Clarice had been waiting for him, he would only have been able to put away momentarily the need he felt for the blond woman. His experience with Jamie had done even less for him because they had both gone through it for entirely the wrong reasons.

He looked down at his crotch and thought that, if and when he finally did get together with Susannah Moore, it would be worth the wait.

He just hoped the wait wouldn't be too much longer.

Ed Blaine and James Butler Hickok had hotel rooms in Springfield's other hotel, which was called the Springfield

House as opposed to the Springfield Hotel where Clint was staying.

Blaine went to bed thinking that they had a pretty good shot at winning the election as long as Hickok listened more to him and Clint Adams than he did to Colonel Nichols.

Maybe the best thing for all concerned would be for Nichols to leave town—one way or another.

Hickok put his guns down by the bed and started to remove his boots. His thoughts went from Susannah Moore to Ed Blaine to Clint Adams and, finally, to the fame promised him by Colonel Nichols.

He owed Blaine because the man had given up his own newspaper career—although it was winding to a close, anyway—to manage his campaign. He didn't owe Susannah Moore anything more than what he gave her in bed and vice versa.

Clint Adams was a new friend, but already a valued one. He hoped that he'd be able to convince the Gunsmith to pin on a star again if he won the election.

As for Nichols—well, he could tell him stories after he was elected just as well as he could before, and then he wouldn't have a campaign to worry about.

That night, Hickok's busy mind never once thought of the name Tutt—either Dave or Jamie.

Both Tutts were thinking about Hickok, however.

Jamie still wanted him, but her feelings were turning more and more toward anger—and most of the anger was because his rejection had forced her into demeaning herself with his friend, Clint Adams.

Dave Tutt was just waiting for the Turner brothers to show up. He figured that it wouldn't take long before a showdown would take place between them and Hickok and then he'd be rid of Hickok for good.

● ● ●

Colonel George Nichols was staying in the same hotel as Clint Adams. As he retired, he thought about Hickok and Clint Adams. Hickok was easy to categorize. He was young, full of himself, an easy mark for a man like himself if not for the stabilizing effect of a man like Ed Blaine. Adams, too, was a stabilizing effect on Hickok, although they were the same age.

Clint Adams had potential. He wasn't as flashy as Hickok, and he didn't have much of an ego to play on, so for the moment there was nothing for Nichols to work with.

Except what he had learned about the man from playing poker with him.

Nichols decided to stay in Springfield for a while longer to collect stories about Wild Bill Hickok and to do some research on Clint Adams, the Gunsmith.

Susannah Moore was also getting ready to go to bed alone. She had half expected Hickok to show up and was actually relieved when he didn't. She and Jim Hickok fit well together in bed, but her mind was elsewhere tonight.

It was on Clint Adams.

He wanted her, she knew. She knew when men wanted her, and she'd been able to see it in his eyes when they'd had dinner together. His loyalty to Hickok had been commendable, but she thought that, given time, she'd be able to overcome it.

Her original intention, after he'd turned her down, had been to ignore him for the rest of the time they were both in town but, surprisingly, she'd been unable to do that. He kept invading her thoughts and, especially after her uninspiring afternoon with Dave Tutt, she wanted Clint Adams more than ever.

She turned down her bed and slid underneath the covers, aware of the tingle between her warm thighs. She had made herself come earlier in the day, after Tutt had left, and it had been less than satisfying. She decided not to do it again. She would just wait for the moment when she and Clint Adams got together.

She could have gone to his hotel room and knocked on his door, but she decided to let him wait a little longer.

Anything worth having is worth waiting for.

# FOURTEEN

Early the following morning, Ethan and Elmo Turner rode into Springfield, Missouri, and put their horses up at the livery. The liveryman had spent most of his night drinking, and as the twins pulled up in front of his stable, he swore off drinking, thinking he was seeing double.

They presented themselves at the door of the Tutts' boardinghouse, which they had inherited from their parents. Jamie answered the door and both Turners thought she was the prettiest thing they'd ever seen.

"Are you gonna talk or just stare?" she asked them.

"Uh," said Ethan, the younger brother.

"Um," said Elmo.

"Well?" Jamie said impatiently.

"We're here to see Dave Tutt," Elmo said finally.

"He's gonna give us some money," Ethan added.

"He's not gonna give us some money, stupid," Elmo said, and then he looked at Jamie and added, "We're gonna work for it."

"Work?" she asked, frowning. "What kind of work could you do for Dave?"

"Do you know Dave?" Ethan asked.

"He's my brother."

"Could you tell him that we're here?" Elmo asked.

For a moment she entertained the thought of inviting them in, but there were other boarders who might not appreciate their presence, so she said, "Wait here." She closed the door and went up to Dave's room, waking him up to tell him that there were two men to see him.

"Who?"

"I didn't get their names," she said, "but they look like a couple of farm boys. They say they're going to work for you, Dave."

"The Turners," he said, throwing back the covers and sitting up in bed. Jamie was always surprised when she saw her brother with his shirt off. If anything, he always seemed to be bigger than she remembered with huge muscular slabs on his chest, shoulders, and arms.

"What kind of work, Dave?"

"Never mind," he said, rubbing his hand briskly over his short hair. "Get breakfast for the house, Jamie. I'll see to them."

She frowned, but knew she'd get nothing out of her brother that he didn't want to give.

"All right."

She left to prepare breakfast, and Dave Tutt dressed and went down to greet the Turners.

He took them into the sitting room where they couldn't be seen or overheard from the kitchen.

"That smells good," Ethan said, sniffing the air.

"Eggs and ham," Elmo said.

"Never mind that," Tutt said, "I didn't invite you here to eat."

The Turners were as tall as Tutt, but combined they might not have matched his body weight. Still, he knew he had to be careful with them. He knew how fast the guns on their hips could be brought into use.

"All right," he said, "let's talk business and then we'll talk about breakfast. Is that fair?"

"Sounds fair to me," Ethan said, nodding. "How about you, Elmo?"

"Sounds fair."

"Have you ever heard of Wild Bill Hickok?"

"Seems to me I've heard that name before," Ethan said. "What about you, Elmo?"

"Ain't he a gunny?"

"He was a scout for the army and he knows how to use a gun," Tutt said.

"What about him?" Ethan asked.

"Are you two fellas afraid of him?"

This time Ethan answered for the both of them. "We ain't afraid of nobody."

"You want us to kill him?" Elmo asked.

"That's exactly what I want you to do."

"Before or after breakfast?" Ethan asked.

"Hold on," Tutt said, "it's not that easy. All I want you to do for now is keep an eye on him, because sooner or later Hickok's gonna come after me, and that's when I want you to take him—if you can."

Ethan looked at Elmo who looked at Dave Tutt and asked, "Does this mean we can eat now?"


Marshal Saul Tucker saw the Turner brothers ride into town and recognized them. For just a moment he considered playing at being a real lawman. The Turners were killers for hire, and if they were in town, it was because somebody had sent for them.

Who had sent for them wasn't the question, though. The question was who were they here for?

Hickok was the only man in town who would rate a couple of killers like the Turners. And maybe Clint Adams, but Adams didn't have any enemies in town. Hickok had Dave

Tutt, and after the Turners had left the livery stable they'd gone straight to the Tutt's boardinghouse. You didn't have to be a genius to figure out what that meant.

The proper thing to do would be to face them and order them out of town. Of course, they might kill him if he tried that.

And then, of course, there was another reason to leave them be. Wild Bill Hickok was his opponent, and if Hickok were gone—or dead—there just wouldn't be any competition at all. You didn't have to be a genius to figure that out.

Marshal Saul Tucker was not the only one to see the Turner brothers ride into Springfield, however.

Up unusually early in the morning due to a cold that was keeping him from sleeping normally of late, Joe Brewer, the bartender at the Deadline Saloon, was looking out his window when the twin killers rode down the main street, and he recognized them right off.

Brewer had seen the Turners in action only last year, and he knew who and what they were. He frowned, wondering what they could be doing in Springfield.

He moved away from the window, puzzling over the Turners' appearance in Springfield. He blew his nose furiously, trying in vain to clear it so he could breathe. After a few moments of thought—something else he was unaccustomed to—he figured, what the hell, at least they'd give him something to talk about while he was tending bar.

# FIFTEEN

There was something in the air the next morning at breakfast in the café, and only two people were aware of it. Clint Adams and Susannah Moore may have been sitting at tables across the room from each other, but they were acutely aware of each other and trying not to show it. In spite of this, Clint felt that this day something would happen between them. Even if he had to force the issue!

Susannah finished breakfast first and left the café and, shortly after, Clint did the same. As he got to the street, she was nowhere in sight. It was too early, anyway. When something happened, it would be later in the day. Maybe even all night. Aware that he was starting to respond to the thought of Susannah Moore, Clint decided to try to walk it off.

Although Marshal Tucker and Joe Brewer were the first to see the Turner brothers in town, it was Clint who first spotted the two brothers with Dave Tutt.

The three men were unaware of the Gunsmith, who frowned as he tried to place the tall twins. From across the street, he didn't realize that they were identical, or he would have known immediately who they were. As it was, he didn't find them out until later that afternoon when he went into the Deadline Saloon for his first drink of the day and some conversation with Joe Brewer.

"Seen Hickok yet today, Joe?"

"Naw," Brewer said, setting a beer down in front of Clint. "I'll bet he's off somewhere talking to that writer."

"I don't think so," Clint said. "Hickok's become pretty serious about this campaign for marshal."

"Well, I hope so," Brewer said. "If he were marshal, I bet he wouldn't allow some of the people who are in this town to stay in this town for long."

Clint frowned as he tried to follow that and asked, "Who do you mean?"

"A couple of real killers who rode into town early today. I saw them because I was up early. I can't sleep too well, you know, what with this cold—"

"Killers?" Clint said, the word triggering something in his brain.

"Yep, two of the worst," Brewer said, "and what's more, they're brothers—"

"The Turner brothers!" Clint said, banging his fist down on the bar.

"You saw them, too?"

"Right after breakfast," Clint said, "only I was too far away to identify them. They were with Dave Tutt."

"I thought I saw them going toward Dave's boarding-house." Leaning on the bar, wiping his nose with the bar rag, Brewer asked, "You suppose they're friends of his?"

"Those two don't have any friends," Clint said. "I'm thinking something else and I don't like it?"

"What's that?" Brewer asked, sniffling.

Changing the subject, Clint asked Brewer, "Does this town have a doctor, Joe?"

"It does."

"Why don't you go and see what he can do about that cold instead of letting your nose drip all over the place? It gets so a fella doesn't even want to have a drink in this place."

"Hey—" Brewer called out, but Clint turned and left the saloon quickly.

His initial intention was to seek out Hickok and warn him that Dave Tutt had imported some talent, but he had second thoughts about that. All that might accomplish would be to send Hickok after those two to run them out of town—or die trying.

He decided instead to go and talk to the marshal, whom he had spoken to only after he and Hickok had disposed of the drifters who'd tried to gun them down. Since then, he felt as if the lawman had been avoiding him, possibly because he was obviously friendly with the man's chief competition for the job.

Clint went to the marshal's office and found Tucker sitting behind his desk with a cup of coffee.

"Adams," the man said, looking up.

"Marshal."

"Something I can do for you?"

The man was in his early forties. He had broad shoulders and seemed more than capable of handling himself, but he also seemed like a man who had become complacent with his lot in life. Clint recalled Ed Blaine's telling him that Tucker had held the job of marshal for a good many years, and it was the opinion of many that perhaps it was time for some new blood.

"You can tell me what you intend to do about the Turner boys."

"The Turners?" Tucker asked, frowning as if trying to place the names.

"The hired killers that Dave Tutt has brought into town," Clint said. "Don't pretend you don't know who the Turner brothers are."

"Oh, the Turner brothers," Tucker said. "Are they in town?"

"You know they are and you also know that Tutt brought them here to gun Hickok."

"I don't know any such thing, lad," Tucker said, "and neither do you. Now, I can't be running every man with a little reputation out of town every time one comes in to town."

"A little reputation?" Clint asked, interrupting the man's speech. "Those fellas have more than a little reputation. Some people kill for money; they kill for fun and don't mind getting paid for it."

"Adams, are you trying to tell me how to do my job?" Tucker demanded.

"Somebody better because you're doing a piss-poor job of it."

"Sure," Tucker said, sneering, "that's what you'd like people to believe because you want your friend Hickok to win the election. Well, let me tell you something, Adams, if I hear you spreading any bad talk about me around town, you're the one I'll run out and not the Turners."

"Are you going to keep an eye on them at least?"

"I don't have to explain to you how I'm going to do my job," the man said, thrusting his chin out. "Now, get out of my office, you're ruining my coffee."

As Clint headed for the door, Tucker called out to him, "And don't let me hear that you were bothering the Tutts. They're two of our finest citizens."

Sure, Clint thought, and two votes for you; Dave Tutt hates Hickok, and Jamie Hickok jilted.

For a moment Clint considered continuing the argument, but then decided against it. He wouldn't put it past the marshal to wait and see if the Turners did kill Hickok because the man would certainly get to keep his job that way.

Could he want to hold on to it that badly?

Outside the marshal's office he paused to consider his next

move. He still didn't want to go to Hickok with the news—yet, anyway—so what he finally decided to do was to try to talk to Dave Tutt or the Turners, whoever he ran into first, and see if he couldn't head off a confrontation between the twin killers and Wild Bill Hickok.

In his concern for his friend, it never dawned on him that he might be setting up just such a confrontation between himself and the Turners.

A twenty-eight-year-old Gunsmith still had a lot to learn.

# SIXTEEN

Rather than wait to run into Tutt or the Turners, Clint decided to go to the Tutt boardinghouse.

His knock was answered by Jamie Tutt, whose face immediately reddened with embarrassment and shame.

"What do you want?" she asked, averting her eyes.

"I want to talk to your brother, Jamie."

"Dave?" she asked in surprise. "What about?"

"I'd rather discuss that with him, Jamie," Clint said. "Would you tell him I'm here?"

"He—" she started to say, but suddenly Tutt loomed behind her, putting a huge hand on her shoulder.

"Let's hear what the man has to say, Jamie. Show him into the sitting room."

Tutt disappeared from view and Jamie said, "All right, follow me."

He followed her into the boardinghouse's sitting room where he was confronted by Dave Tutt and the Turner brothers. The three of them were standing in the center of the room, Tutt between the other two men.

The first thing Clint noticed about the Turners was how identical they were. Both were tall and thin and badly in need of a haircut, shave, and bath. And then he noticed that they weren't identical in every way. One of them wore his Colt on his right hip, while the other wore his on his left.

"This is Ethan Turner," Dave Tutt said, indicating the lefty, "and this is Elmo."

"I'm Elmo," the lefty said, correcting Tutt's error.

"And I'm Ethan," the other brother said.

"I'm Clint Adams."

Elmo frowned and said, "I read about you—"

"They call you the Gunsmith, don't they?" Ethan asked.

"Yeah, some people do."

"Never mind that," Dave Tutt said. "What do you want, Adams?"

"I want to try to avoid any unnecessary bloodshed, Tutt."

"How?"

"By convincing you that bringing these two here was wrong."

"Wrong? You or Hickok can decide at any moment to kill me, Adams. You think I stand a chance against either of you?"

"That's nonsense."

"Is it? Maybe for you, but not to Hickok. He's wanted me dead for a long time."

"That's between you and him."

"So you say," Tutt replied. "I say I have the right to bring in all the help I need to stay alive and that's just what I've done."

"Sure, two killers who'd pull the trigger on anyone you pointed your finger at."

"For money, Adams," Tutt added, "and I could point my finger at you right now and they'd cut you down."

"You won't, though."

"Why not?"

"Because then you'd have to explain what happened."

"You came in here, started making threats, and drew on us," Tutt said with a shrug. "We were forced to kill you in self-defense."

"Three against one?"

"Everybody knows you've got a reputation, Adams."

"Still, only a fool would draw on three men," Clint said, "and only a bigger fool would gun me down, Tutt, in front of a witness." With that they all looked at the fifth person in the room, Jamie Tutt. The young woman looked bewildered and more than a little frightened.

"Go into the kitchen, Jamie," Tutt said to her.

"Dave, is this all true? Are these men hired killers you brought here to kill James?"

"They're men I brought here to protect me from Hickok," he explained. "Now, go into the kitchen."

"I don't think I've done any good here, Tutt," Clint said. "I had hoped I'd be able to talk some sense into you, but I can see that's useless. You want bloodshed and I suppose you're going to get it."

Tutt tensed, as if he expected the Gunsmith to draw on him, but instead Clint backed his way out of the sitting room, while the three men watched him warily.

When he was gone, Tutt whirled on Jamie and said, "Damn it, I told you to go into the kitchen!"

"So you could kill him without any witnesses?"

"I wasn't going to kill him—ah, the hell with it. I don't have to explain anything to you, Jamie. You're just a woman and you don't understand."

"Dave Tutt—"

He took a step toward her and she shrank back, fearing a blow. "Now, go into the kitchen and get lunch ready for our boarders." She backed away from him until she bumped into the kitchen door and then fled through it.

Ethan and Elmo Turner looked at each other, and then Elmo turned to Dave Tutt and asked, "Does this mean we can eat now?"

Instead of starting lunch as her brother had ordered, Jamie

Tutt ran out the back door and around the house to intercept Clint Adams.

"Clint!"

"Jamie," he said, turning, "you shouldn't be out here."

"Everything you said was true, wasn't it? My brother brought those killers here?"

"I'm afraid so, Jamie."

"We have to tell the marshal," she said. "Maybe he can get them to leave before—"

"I've already tried that, Jamie."

"And?"

"If the Turners are here to kill Hickok, Marshal Tucker is all for it. It'll make keeping his job easier."

"But that's awful. He's the law!"

"Yeah," Clint said, "and that's what's awful."

She looked back at the house nervously and said, "I—I have to get back before Dave notices I'm gone. I just wanted you to know—I had nothing to do with bringing those men here. I didn't know anything about it."

"I know you didn't, Jamie. Go ahead, get back to the house."

She hesitated a moment, touching her hair, and said, "Maybe another time we can . . . uh, maybe we can try again. You know . . ."

"Yeah, I know. Go on, now, before he sees that you're gone."

She ran back around the house and out of sight, and Clint decided finally that he had no other choice but to go to Hickok and warn him.

# SEVENTEEN

Clint found Hickok in his hotel room with Ed Blaine discussing the campaign. Wild Bill listened patiently while Clint relayed to him the information about the Turners and Marshal Tucker's attitude.

"None of it surprises me," Hickok said, when Clint finished.

"Why not?" Blaine asked.

"Hell, with me dead the job's Tucker's again for the asking" Hickok explained, "and as for the Turners, it figures that Dave Tutt would bring someone else in. He hasn't got the guts to face me himself, not even with Jim Courtwright backing him."

"What's Courtwright's story?" Blaine inquired.

Hickok shrugged and said, "He's always been with Tutt, as long as I've known them."

"Which is how long?"

"We met during the war," Hickok said and didn't elaborate any further.

"What are you going to do about the Turners, Jim?" Clint asked.

"Nothing," Hickok said, shrugging again.

"Tutt's going to wait for you to make a move," Clint said.

"He's gonna have a long wait," Hickok said, "and he'll get tired. Sooner or later he'll get tired and send the Turners after me, and after I finish with them, I'll have every excuse I need to finish him as well.''

"Not if you're marshal by that time," Blaine said. "If you're wearing a badge by that time, you'll have to handle it differently.''

Hickok looked at Ed Blaine then and said, "Whether I'm wearing a badge or not, Ed, I'll handle situations my own way. I'm not gonna change.''

"Jim—''

"Relax, Ed," Hickok said, patting the man heavily on the shoulder. "Come on, I'll spring for drinks.''

Saul Tucker looked up as his office door opened, afraid that it might be Clint Adams again.

It was Dave Tutt.

"Hello, Dave.''

"Marshal.''

Tutt walked over to the lawman's stove and helped himself to some coffee. He took it with him and sat across from Tucker's desk.

"I guess you must have heard I got some company in town,'' Tutt said.

"I heard," Tucker said. "The Turners, isn't it?''

"Yep," Tutt said, sipping his coffee. He made a face and put the cup down on the marshal's desk. "How do you feel about that, Saul?''

Tucker shrugged and said, "Long as they don't cause any trouble I got no argument with them.''

"You know, if they should happen to have to kill Hickok—you know, in self-defense—that'll leave you your job with no problem—that is until the next election.''

"You saying Hickok will beat me in the election?'' Tucker demanded.

"I'm asking why take that chance?'' Tucker said.

"You're saying that you don't want me in the way when push comes to shove between Hickok and your hired killers."

"Nobody said anything about hired killers," Tutt said, frowning.

"Don't play games with me, Dave," Tucker said. "Just make sure that your hired killers don't miss and that it looks damn well like self-defense or a fair fight because if not, then I'd have to do my job."

"Sure," Tutt said, standing up, "sure. Whatever you say."

Tutt left, glad that Springfield had a marshal who was so selective about how and when he did his job.

Clint, Hickok, and Blaine found themselves a table and set about sharing a bottle of whiskey.

"If it comes to it," Clint said after a while, "you won't have to stand alone against the Turners, Courtwright, and Tutt."

"Well," Hickok said, filling their glasses again, "I'd be a fool to turn down your help with the Turners. They've got themselves the kind of reputation you don't come by by accident. As for Tutt and Courtwright, though, they're mine and I owe them too much to share them."

"Why do we have to discuss this?" Blaine argued. "Maybe it won't even come to that."

Hickok looked at Blaine and grinned. "You're a good campaign manager, Ed, but you don't know shit about human nature. Dave Tutt and I are on the same path going in different directions. Sooner or later we're gonna bump heads and neither one of us is gonna back down. That's just the way it is."

Blaine looked to Clint Adams for help, but there wasn't any to be had. Clint just shrugged his shoulders and poured another drink. He was facing the door and the rest of the room—as was Hickok. Blaine was seated with his back facing the door.

"Company," Clint said. Hickok had already seen them and Blaine turned around to take a look.

"Jesus," he said, staring at the Turner twins, "you can't tell them apart."

Clint exchanged glances with Hickok and said, "I can."

The Turners went to the bar for a bottle and then took it to a table in the opposite corner of the room. They sat so they both could see the door and the rest of the room.

"Bill," Clint said.

"Yeah?"

"You got a deck of cards?"

"Sure," Hickok said, producing a fresh deck. "You wanna play now?"

"Yep," Clint said, taking the cards and standing up, "but not with you."

# EIGHTEEN

Clint carried the cards to the table Ethan and Elmo Turner were sitting at and asked, "You fellas poker players?"

"We sure are," Elmo said, "ain't we, Ethan?"

"Sure are," Ethan said, "and for a change we got money to play with."

"Tutt give you an advance, did he?"

"He sure did," Elmo said.

Clint sat down and broke the seal on the fresh deck.

"You got a lot of guts, sitting down here to play cards with us," Ethan said.

"Why? You fellas especially good poker players?"

"A lot of guts," Elmo said.

Clint dealt out five cards each and then glanced at his.

"You boys have got quite a reputation," he said, eyeing them over the spread cards.

"Guess so," Ethan said. Elmo frowned as he concentrated on his cards.

"Your bet, Elmo," Clint said to the lefty.

Elmo looked at Clint and asked, "How'd you know I was Elmo?"

Clint grinned at him and said, "I can tell you apart."

He didn't believe it, but it appeared that neither brother was able to figure out how.

"It's your bet, Elmo," he said again.

"A dollar," Elmo said.

"Ethan?" Clint said.

"I'll see my brother a dollar."

Clint looked at his hand and said, "I'll raise it a dollar."

"Call," the Turner brothers said, throwing in their money in turn.

"How many?" Clint asked Elmo.

"Three."

"Ethan?"

"Three."

"I'll take two."

He dealt out the cards and then waited for Elmo, who was the opener.

"A dollar," Elmo said, tossing it in.

"I call," Ethan said.

"I raise."

Elmo frowned at Clint, peered intently at his cards, and then tossed in his dollar. His brother did the same.

"Three queens," Clint said, laying them down.

"That beats me," Elmo said, throwing his cards down so Clint could see the pair of kings he'd opened with and not improved on. Ethan also tossed his cards down, face up, showing a pair of eights.

He wondered if they used their guns better than they played cards.

"What's he trying to do?" Blaine asked Hickok.

"He's feeling them out, and maybe he's keeping them from looking over here too much," Hickok said.

"They won't come after you until Tutt sends them, right?"

"They're not too smart, Ed," Clint said. "That makes them unpredictable and dangerous."

"And Clint's sitting over there with them."

"And, from the way it looks, taking their money," Hickok said, grinning.

They were playing for a few hours, Clint talking, asking questions, listening carefully to the answers, trying to find out everything he could about Ethan and Elmo Turner.

"So you boys think you can take Hickok, huh?" Clint asked, dealing out another hand. He'd just taken eight straight from them.

"We can take anybody," Ethan said.

"As long as we're together," Elmo added.

Clint paused as he was dealing the cards, then finished dealing what would be the last hand.

He'd finally heard something he could use.

After that hand was over, Clint said, "That's it for me, boys, but we'll do this again. I want to give you a chance to get your money back."

They couldn't argue with that. He was leaving a winner, but he was promising them a chance to get it back. As dimwitted as they were, even the Turners recognized that as fair.

"Okay," Ethan said, sitting back.

"Can I get you boys another bottle?" Clint asked.

"Naw," Elmo said, "one's enough for us."

"We gotta go," Ethan said, and they slid their chairs back and stood up. Clint moved himself so that he was standing between them and Hickok.

"See you fellas around."

Elmo started for the door, but stopped when he realized that Ethan wasn't following.

"You're a good card player, Adams," Ethan said, his tone menacing. "But don't try to go up against us with a gun." Just for a moment Clint wondered if the brother's moron act was just that, an act, but he dismissed the thought as unacceptable. For them to be fast with their guns *and* smarter than they appeared was too frightening a thought to entertain.

"Together, we can take anybody," Ethan Turner finished.

That was the second time one of them had expressed that idea.

"I'll remember, boys," he promised.

When Clint returned to the table where Hickok and Blaine were waiting, both men looked at him expectantly.

"Well?" Blaine asked.

"Well," Clint said, "I won fifty dollars."

"I don't mean that—"

"Easy, Ed," Hickok said, putting his hand on his campaign manager's arm.

"Sorry," Blaine said. He was not only worried that the Turners might present a danger to Hickok's campaign, but to his life as well.

"Did you find out anything helpful?" Hickok asked Clint.

"Yep," Clint said, pouring himself a drink from the bottle on the table. He drank it down, then regarded both men and said, "I found out that together they can take anyone—they think."

"What does that mean?" Blaine asked.

"It means that they are convinced that they're unbeatable together."

"That helps?"

"It does if it's true," Clint said. "Look, I'm going to get some shut-eye because in the morning I want to do some research."

"But I still don't understand—" Blaine was saying as Clint stood up to leave.

Hickok waved Clint away, and as the Gunsmith headed for the door, he heard Wild Bill saying, "Let me explain it to you, Ed . . ."

# NINETEEN

As he reached the Springfield Hotel, Clint realized that he was just a little bit drunk. He navigated the steps to the second floor, and as he headed toward his room, his mind snapped back to his earlier thoughts about Susannah Moore. His penis immediately swelled erect. He stopped for a moment, and then he decided to go and take a bath instead—probably a cold one.

It was late enough so that he wasn't concerned that someone else might be using the hotel's bathing facilities. He grabbed a towel and went down through the lobby, passed the dozing clerk, and down the hall to the hotel's bathhouse. It was separated into two areas, one for undressing and one for bathing. He stripped, slung his gunbelt over his naked shoulders, and then entered the room where the bathtubs were, his raging erection preceding him.

As he entered he heard water and then became aware of someone's humming—before he saw her seated in the tub with her back to him. He stared at her, smooth and glistening, and tried to decide whether to back out of the room or simply clear his throat to announce his presence. Then his left foot struck a small wooden stool, knocking it over.

Her head whipped around quickly, eyes wide. When she saw that it was him, however, a slow, wide grin spread out over her face. Frankly she inspected his erect penis and obviously approved of what she saw.

"Well, what brings you here?" he asked.

"It's late," she said. "I figured I'd be able to take a bath undisturbed."

"That's what I thought, too. But this isn't your hotel," he said.

"I changed hotels. I wanted at least a little distance from Hickok," she answered.

"Well, I let you finish—" he started to say.

"Oh, don't let me stop you," she said. Then looking at the gunbelt slung over his shoulder, she added, "Unless you're afraid of me. You're not afraid of me, are you?"

"Of course not," he said calmly, even though he was angry. His anger stemmed from the look on her face and her attitude. He was sure that she felt he'd never get out of this room without having sex with her, and he resented her feeling she could manipulate him.

"You'll have to get your own water."

"That's no problem," he said, removing the gunbelt from his shoulder.

She watched, her hands on the side of the tub and her chin perched on her hands, as he filled a tub, walking back and forth with the water buckets.

Clint, in turn, made an effort not to look her way while he was carrying the water. He wouldn't have seen much, anyway, since most of her was submerged. All he was aware of was her hair tied on top of her head with a pink ribbon.

This wasn't going to work, he thought as he dumped the last bucket of water into the tub. The whole purpose of this bath was to ease his need for her, and now she was right in the next tub, gloriously naked and mocking him, and his need was becoming even more urgent.

He pulled a chair over to the tub, hung his gunbelt over the back, and then climbed into the tub, surprised by how cold the water was. What surprised him more was that his penis, totally unaffected by the cold, remained erect and was even pulsing.

"How is it?" Susannah asked.

"Cold."

"Mine was, too, but if you sit in it long enough, it starts to warm up."

"You've been here for a while?"

"I like long baths."

"I guess you're just about ready to leave, then," he said hopefully.

"Do you want me to leave?"

"It's up to you," he said, shrugging his shoulders as if it was of no concern to him.

"All right, then," she said, bracing her hands on the side of the tub, "I'll leave."

She pushed herself to her feet and he watched in awe. She stood up and the water cascaded down her body—over her firm breasts, rolling off her nipples in twin rivulets. Her hips were wide, her thighs solid, and as she stepped out of the tub, she presnted her backside to him, showing it to be firm and possibly the loveliest he'd ever had the pleasure to see.

He was painfully aware of his erection which, despite the coldness of the water, seemed full to bursting. He had not taken the time to fill the tub all the way, and the swollen head of his penis broke the surface of the water.

She turned then and faced him, showing him her smile again.

"I'm leaving," she said, putting her hands on her hips and posing for him.

"Fine," he said, thinking that bitch knows how beautiful she is!

"Maybe you need someone to scrub your back, though?" she asked, approaching the tub.

"No, that's all right—" he started to say and then he

brought himself up short. What am I doing? he thought. What did it matter if she thought that she was manipulating him into sex? In fact, she probably still thought that he did not want to touch her because of his loyalty to his friend.

His anger faded into satisfaction as he watched her walk across the room, firm breasts just barely bouncing as she moved, secure in the feeling that she could tease him.

He had felt all along that if something were going to happen between them it would be today. And now it would.

When she reached the tub, her eyes widened as she saw the head of his penis sticking up from the water, as if it were floating there.

"Oh, it looks like something instead of your back needs immediate attention."

"No," he said, still playing the part of the reluctant lover, "it's all right—"

"And you need soap," she said. She turned and trotted back to her tub and bent over to reach for the soap, giving him a tantalizing view of her pale behind and her pink pubic mound.

She came back with the soap and dropped it into the water, where it immediately sank from view.

"Oh, how clumsy," she said, dropping to her knees. "I'll find it for you."

She plunged her hand into the water and grabbed a handful of his testicles.

"Oh, I'm sorry," she said. She gave his jewels a light squeeze and then continued her supposed search for the soap. This time when she closed her hand it was around his rigid cock and he closed his eyes, afraid he'd come right there and then.

"I'm sorry," she said again. "Did I hurt you?"

"No."

"Do I detect your resolve weakening," she asked, sliding

her hand up and down his pole.

He looked into her eyes then, reached out, took a handful of her right breast, and said, "Oh, yes."

"Good," she said.

She reached into the water with her other hand and, while fondling his erection with one hand, she teased his testicles with the other.

Looking at her, Clint could see that the cool air in the room was drying her off and giving her goose bumps.

"You're going to get all wet again," he warned her, putting one moist hand behind her head.

"I don't mind."

As if to prove her point, she positioned herself so that she could reach him with her mouth and ran her tongue over the crown of his penis.

Clint put his right hand on the back of her neck, said, "Oh, no!"—and pushed her face down into the water playfully.

She reared back, pulling her head out of the water, coughing and falling onto her butt. Water streamed from her face, and her hair came loose as she shook her head.

Clint stood up, got out of the tub, and stood over her, straddling her as she attempted to push herself up to a sitting position. His penis was still rigid and pulsing.

"What's the matter?" he asked her. "Get a little wet?"

"Bastard!"

Her knee came up like a shot, but Clint turned quickly enough and caught it on the inside of his thigh. She was strong, and he'd have a bruise there to prove it, but she wasn't as strong as he was.

"You bastard—" she shouted again, coming up off the floor at him with amazing speed. She was trying to push him back so that he'd fall into the tub, giving her revenge for the dunking he'd given her.

He slid his arms around her, pinning her arms to her side,

turned with the force of her charge in order to retain his
balance, and then gently lowered her to the floor again—with
himself on top.

"Let me up," she said, struggling weakly—only half-
serious—against his superior strength and weight.

"First, I'm going to give you what you've been wanting,"
he said, shifting so that he could pin her arms to the floor with
his hands.

She felt his lips brushing her neck and moving down over
her breasts. His rigid manhood poked at her moist, pink love
portal.

"Well," she said, closing her eyes and grinning, "it's
about time!"

# TWENTY

Later, while they lay together in his bed taking a well-deserved rest, Susannah thought about what had happened in the bathhouse.

After Clint pushed her to the floor, she felt his lips moving over her neck and breasts, nibbling at her nipples while his hard cock was pushing to gain entry. The helplessness that she initially felt quickly turned to excitement. She'd never been totally dominated by a man before, and the sensation made her suddenly gushingly moist. His rigid manhood pierced her deeply, the penetration made even bolder by their lying on an unyielding floor rather than a mattress.

As he pounded into her, still pinning her arms to the floor, she became dizzy and breathless. She'd wrapped her legs around his waist and moved her hips in unison with his, and when they came together, she thought that she would black out.

When he released her, she slapped him across the face and said, "That was wonderful, you bastard. Let's go to your room."

They dressed, went to his room, immediately fell into bed, and made love again . . . slowly . . .

"Are you rested?" he asked, bringing her back to the present.

"God, yes," she said, turning toward him. He stopped her, though, and pushed her on her back.

"I want to taste you," he said, and slid down so that his head was between her legs.

God, she thought, the man is incredible.

Clint flicked his tongue out, making his first sampling quick. Her taste lingered on his tongue and again he pressed his lips to her, kissing deeply and then thrusting his tongue all the way inside her. Her thighs tensed and she lifted her hips to him. He slid his hands beneath her so he could cup her firm buttocks and press his face firmly. As he began to lick, her hands came down and cupped his head, and she started to move her hips, rubbing herself into the pressure of his lapping tongue.

"Oh, God . . ." she moaned. "Yes, lick me, lick me . . . suck me now."

He used his tongue to tease her until she went rigid, and then he pursed his lips and began to suck. She made a high keening sound, which graduated into a hoarse moaning, and her hips began gyrating up and down, making it hard for him to hold her buttocks and keep his mouth in place.

As his tongue and lips worked on her, she moved her hands from his head so she could grab her pillow and push her face into it. She bit down on the pillow and screamed into it as he unmercifully continued to tongue her, holding her down so that she couldn't escape.

She started to feel dizzy again as she felt her orgasm building, slowly at first and then suddenly rising up to take hold of her. She came and he continued to lick her.

"Please," she said, "please, fuck me now."

He pulled his face free of her, and as he raised himself over her, the air touched the moistness on his face, making it feel cool and then drying it. He plunged into the sweet, hot depths of her again and she wrapped her arms and legs around him.

Then she was coming again as he drove himself to his own orgasm. And then again, as he achieved his.

"You've done things to me tonight that no man has ever done."

"And?"

"I'm still trying to decide whether I liked it all."

"Really? I don't have any complaints."

She said, "Oh, I enjoyed most of it, but being helpless, being dominated . . . that's something that will take some getting used to for me."

"I don't usually dominate a woman I'm with," he said. "When I'm with a woman, we usually . . . satisfy each other, work together to give each other pleasure . . ."

"And with me?"

"With you it's a battle, I think, to see who dominates."

She stared thoughtfully at him for a moment, propping herself up on an elbow. "I think you're right," she said. "I usually dominate my men and this was the first time I've ever been dominated."

"Then you've got another first coming," he said, drawing her to him.

"What's that?"

"Cooperation," he said, kissing her warmly.

"So that was cooperation, huh?" she said a little while later.

"That was it."

She sighed heavily and said, "I think you've ruined me for other men, Clint Adams."

"I hope not."

She turned her head on the pillow to look at his profile and said, "You were supposed to say I hope so."

He turned his head to look at her and said, "Susannah—"

"No, never mind," she said, holding her hand up. "I'm not a clingy female and I won't let you turn me into one, even if you are an exceptional man . . . and an exceptional lover . . . I'm not making this any easier for myself."

"Susannah—"

"I'm teasing," she said, rolling over so she could lay her right arm across his chest and snuggle up to him.

"All I want," she said, "is a place to sleep for the night."

"That I can offer you," he said, but when he looked at her, he saw that she had already fallen asleep. Not that he could blame her. He was totally exhausted himself. He'd never known that such nice things could happen when you set out to take a late night bath.

In the morning they made love slowly and with a lot of cooperation. Then he watched her get dressed.

"Your turn," she said, sitting on the bed.

"It sure won't be as nice as watching you," he warned her.

"I'll be the judge of that, sir," she said, seating herself on the bed. "Go ahead, dress."

He washed up using the pitcher and basin on the dresser and then got dressed self-consciously while she watched him closely.

"What's the matter?" she asked. "Never had a woman watch you get dressed before?"

"Not really," he replied. "How'd I do?"

"Great," she said with mock seriousness. "Did you know that you put your pants on one leg at a time, just like everybody else?"

"Well, that's a relief to know."

"Talking about relief," she said, "you're not going to have any trouble with Jim Hickok over this, you know."

"Oh, I'm not worried about that," he said, strapping on his gun.

"You know that?" she said. "Did you ask him for permission?"

"Not really," he said. "The subject of him and you just came up in conversation."

"And?"

"And he told me to go ahead and take my best shot," he said, smiling at her.

She grinned, got up, and walked to the door. When she had it open, she looked at him and said, "Well, Mr. Adams, you certainly did do that," and she left.

# TWENTY-ONE

Clint didn't know what kind of a newspaper the *Springfield Gazette* was, but he was about to find out that morning. He went directly to the office of the *Gazette* after breakfast. There was an elderly man attending to the press and Clint asked to see the editor.

"You're lookin' at him, sonny," the man said, smiling to reveal toothless gums.

"You're the editor."

"Walter Lovely," the man said and added, "and I'll thank you not to make any remarks about my name."

"No, of course not," Clint said, but the man couldn't stop him from thinking of a few.

"Ain't as old as I look, either," the man said, "just lost my teeth early."

Even if that were true, he couldn't be a day under sixty-five.

"I've been the editor of this here rag since I started it. What can I do for you?"

"How extensive is your coverage of events outside Springfield?"

"Depends."

"On what?"

The man picked up an ink-stained rag and began to wipe

his hands with it. "I cover things that happen in Springfield first, but if I find out somethin' big, I use it."

"Do you just cover Missouri?"

"I print anything big, sonny," Lovely said, "even if I got to take it out of somebody else's paper. What's this all about?"

"I'd like to look at some of your old issues."

"Sure I keep 'em," the old man said, jerking his head and adding, "out back. What are you interested in?"

"The Turner boys."

"Ethan and Elmo?" The man made a face and said, "A bad pair, mean and stupid; that's a dangerous combination."

"I agree."

"Well, come on back, then, and I'll show you where the stuff is. How far back you wanna go?"

"A couple of years, I guess."

"Well, I guess you're lucky I don't put out a daily," Lovely said.

Clint found what he was looking for in a half dozen issues of the *Gazette*. He read the articles, memorized the facts he needed, and then thanked Walter Lovely for the help.

"You was back there a few hours," Lovely said. "Did you find what you wanted?"

"I sure did, Mr. Lovely."

"Well, then, perhaps you'd care to make a small donation to the operation of this newspaper."

Clint regarded Mr. Lovely for a few moments and came to the decision that if he did make a donation it certainly would go into the newspaper and not toward a bottle of whiskey.

"I'd be happy to, Mr. Lovely."

"Bless you, lad," Lovely said, holding out a wrinkled, bony hand, "a true believer in the freedom of the press, you are."

●　　●　　●

Clint found Hickok coming out of his hotel and said, "I'll buy you lunch."

"Lunch? I ain't had breakfast yet."

"No early campaigning today?"

"Thank God, no. Got to talk to some people this afternoon, though. Jesus, what did you do to your hands?"

Clint looked down at his hands and for the first time noticed that they were covered with newspaper ink.

"Come on, I'll buy you something to eat and tell you all about it."

They stopped at a trough so Clint could clean his hands and then they went on to the café where they were waited on by Clarice who was sweet as pie to Hickok.

"What'd you do to Clarice?" Hickok asked.

"What does a man to do a woman?"

"Woman or women?" Hickok asked.

"Uh—" Clint said.

Hickok laughed and said, "No wonder she's mad at you."

It was true that Hickok had given Clint his blessing with Susannah, but the Gunsmith still did not feel he should volunteer the information that he'd slept with both Jamie and Susannah, women Hickok himself had been seeing.

After Clarice had brought Hickok breakfast and Clint lunch, Wild Bill said, "Now, what was it you wanted to tell me about?"

"The Turners."

"I know all about the Turners, Clint—"

"No, you don't," Clint said, interrupting him. "Do you know that they've killed anyone they've ever faced together?"

"Not for a fact, but I could have told you that was likely."

"And that they've succeeded at anything they've ever done together?"

"What are you getting at? You want me to up and leave town to avoid them?"

"That's not my point, Bill," Clint said. "I've just come from reading back issues of the *Springfield Gazette*, specifically articles about the Turner boys."

"And?"

"And did you know that on occasion each has tried to handle something alone and each has always failed."

"Like what things?"

"Elmo tried to settle accounts with a fella once, and the fella beat him half to death. Later, Elmo and Ethan tracked the fella down and killed him and some friends he was with easy as you please. The same failure to succeed alone happened to Ethan at least once that I know of."

Hickok forked some ham and eggs into his mouth and regarded Clint thoughtfully while he chewed.

"I knew last night that you'd found out something playing cards with those two."

"Right," Clint said. "They can take anybody as long as they're together. It's funny, Bill, but maybe it's not so odd. I've heard of cases of twins knowing what each other was thinking and feeling what the other feels. In this case maybe Ethan and Elmo are like two parts of the same person. One can't function without the other—at least, not on the same level that they do as a pair."

"So when the time comes all we got to do is make sure they're apart."

"Right."

"How do we do that? Those two are just about joined at the hip, and if what you say is true, then they've probably learned their lesson. They're not about to let so much as a breeze come between them."

"Well, that's just something we're going to have to figure

out,'' Clint said and then attacked his own meal. Reading old newspapers had made him hungry.

"You got any whores in this town?" Clint asked Hickok over coffee.

"You run out of women already?" Hickok asked, grinning.

"They're not for me, Bill."

"For the Turners?" Hickok asked. When Clint nodded, Hickok said, "I don't think you could pay a whore enough to get near them."

"We could get them to talk to them, couldn't we?" Clint asked. "String them along until the time came when we needed to separate them?"

"And how would we know when that was?"

"Let's take one step at a time, Bill," Clint said. "Do you know any whores in town?"

"There are a few," Hickok said, "and I might know one . . . or two . . . or three of them."

"Let's talk to them," Clint said.

"How much do we offer them?"

"That depends on how far we want them to go—or how far they are willing to go."

"If they see the Turners before," Hickok said, "it's going to cost us a bundle."

Clint grinned and said, "We'll just call it a campaign expense."

"Ed will love that."

"This comes under the heading of keeping you alive," Clint said, "and that damn well is a campaign expense."

"By golly," Hickok said, "it is."

The first woman's name was Mandy Roberts, and she

worked in the Deadline Saloon sometimes. When Hickok
brought Clint to her room and introduced them, he realized
that he had seen her there once or twice.

"Both of you?" Mandy asked after the introductions were
made. "That's gonna cost double."

She wasn't bad looking, although a little washed out.
Brown hair, a plump little figure with big round breasts, a
full-lipped, bee-stung mouth, she'd sure appeal to a rider just
off the trail—or to someone like Elmo and Ethan Turner.

"No, you don't understand—" Clint started, but she cut
him off, executing a couple of quick steps and bumping into
him with her bouncy breasts.

"Maybe your friend just wants to watch?" she asked. "I
saw you at the Deadline. I could make you feel really good,"
she said, putting her hand on his crotch. Of its own accord his
penis began to swell and she rubbed it, her eyes shining. "We
could have a really good time together, you know what I
mean?"

Over her shoulder he could see Hickok suppressing laugh-
ter. "Uh, yeah, I know what you mean. Actually, though,
we're not here for ourselves, Miss Roberts—"

"Mandy," she said, wetting her plump lips with a moist,
pink tongue.

"Right," he said, "but we're not here for ourselves,
Mandy."

"You're not?" she asked, pushing her bottom lip out. He
thought that it was probably a look designed to make him
drop his pants. When that didn't happen, she stared at him for
a few moments, then dropped her hand, and took two steps
back. "Then what are you wasting my time for?"

"We have a proposition for you and for one other girl,"
Clint said.

They had decided to approach one whore and, if she were

interested, have her bring a second girl into it. If not, they'd go on to the second girl themselves.

"Mister, what's on your mind?"

He proceeded to tell her just what was on their minds.

"She went for it," Hickok said as they left Mandy Roberts's room.

"You surprised?"

Hickok shrugged. "It's a little depressing, though," Hickok added, shaking his head.

"What is?"

"When you asked her if she wanted to see the Turners first before she agreed, she said, 'A man is a man.' How do you like being lumped in with Elmo and Ethan Turner?"

Clint thought about it a moment and then said, "It's a little depressing."

"It's depressing as hell!" Hickok said.

Later that evening over drinks at the Deadline, Clint said, "I think I've got an idea."

"About what?"

"About how we'll know when Tutt is going to use the Turners."

"How?"

"By getting information from someone inside his boardinghouse."

"You want to put somebody inside—"

"No," Clint said, "we've already got somebody inside the house, Bill."

"We do?" Hickok asked, frowning. He thought it over for a few moments then asked, "Who?"

"Jamie."

● ● ●

The next day Clint managed to isolate Jamie Tutt and put the question to her.

"You want me to spy on my brother?"

"Actually," Clint said, trying to find another way to put it, "I want you to spy on the Turner brothers."

"Those two!" She spat, the disgust she felt showing plainly on her pretty face.

"Your brother brought them here, Jamie, but that doesn't mean he can control them. I want to know anything what anyone says or does—your brother, Courtwright, or the Turners—that might tell me that they're ready to go after Hickok or me." Maybe if she thought she was helping him she'd go through with it.

Clint had managed to catch Jamie as she was coming out of a dress shop on a side street and convinced her to sneak up to his room with him for a talk where they wouldn't be seen.

Now she paced the room, going over his request in her mind. "Dave hasn't been treating me very well lately," she said, as much to herself as to him, "but he's still my brother. I can't betray him—"

"I'm not asking you to betray anyone, Jamie."

"And I can't help Jim Hickok," she continued, "not after the way he treated me." She glared at him boldly and he moved closer to her, so he could take her by the shoulders.

"Jamie, all I'm asking you to do is help me keep anyone from dying—anyone!"

She stared at him for a moment and then her features softened. "You know, I thought maybe you were bringing me up here for another reason."

"Oh?" he asked, smiling. "What reason could that be?"

"I thought you might want to try again, Clint—and I wouldn't be so damned talkative this time."

"Jamie," Clint said, "one thing has nothing to do with the other. You and I are not exchanging favors."

"No, of course not," she said. She chewed her lip, going over it again, and then nodded. "All right. I'll keep my ears open, but I'll only tell you what I think you need to know—and I'm not doing this to help Hickok. I want that understood. This is for you and for Dave. I'm afraid of those Turner brothers and I'm afraid that they'll get Dave killed."

"All right, then. We have a bargain."

"Yes," she said, tilting her chin. He placed his finger beneath it and kissed her, softly at first and then with increasing ardor.

True to her word, she talked less and moaned and groaned a lot more.

# TWENTY-TWO

For the next two days everybody went about his business. James Butler Hickok and Ed Blaine worked on the campaign. Marshal Saul Tucker worked on his, which meant being seen a lot with his badge. Dave and Jamie Tutt ran their boardinghouse, which meant that Jamie did the cooking and cleaning, and Dave collected the rent. Jim Courtwright had no business. He lived in the Tutt boardinghouse for free because he was the only friend Dave Tutt had.

The Turners shared a room in the boardinghouse, but did not have their meals with the rest of the guests. Dave Tutt didn't want them scaring the rest of the guests away, and the Turners felt they were being treated special.

They also felt they were being treated special by a couple of whores named Mandy and Pat. Everytime they went to the Green Branch, those two ladies gave them looks and smiles, and occasionally they'd brush a hip against them. Pretty soon, Elmo told Ethan, it would be more than a hip.

"Don't get nervous," Courtwright told Dave Tutt.

"Sure," Tutt said, "That's so easy for you to say."

They were seated in the sitting room of the Tutt boardinghouse. It was between breakfast and lunch, so most of the boarders were out and Jamie was upstairs cleaning.

"Hickok's got it in for you, too, you know," Tutt told Courtwright.

"I'm not so sure about that anymore, Dave."

"What?" Tutt snapped, not believing what he'd just heard.

"He's had his chances, Dave, and he hasn't taken them. Maybe he's forgotten—"

"Hickok doesn't forget, Jim!" Tutt shouted.

"You're getting nervous, Dave," Courtwright said again. "If Hickok's waiting for anything he's waiting for you—for us—to get nervous and make a mistake."

"I'm not making any mistakes, Jim," Tutt said. "I'm just gonna turn the Turners loose. Hey, get that? I'm a poet—turn the Turners loose."

Courtwright frowned at his friend, wondering if the pressure of sharing a town with Wild Bill Hickok wasn't starting to get to him. Maybe they should just pick up and leave—maybe he should just pick up and leave. After all, he didn't own anything except what was on his back.

"Dave, not yet."

Tutt stared at his friend and then said, "I'm sorry, Jim, but I can't wait anymore. Within the next couple of days, Hickok's a dead man." With that Tutt started from the room, heading for the stairs.

On the stairs Jamie Tutt heard her brother approaching and almost panicked until she remembered that she was in her own house.

She stood up straight, held the towels in her hands tightly, and waited. As she saw her brother's foot come into view, she started walking down the steps, timing it just right.

"Jamie," he said, almost bumping into her as he started up the steps.

"Hello, Dave," she said. He moved aside so she could step down and then went past her and up the stairs two at a time.

Jamie put her towels away and, passing Courtwright in the sitting room, said, "I have to do some shopping."

He wondered why she would tell him that?

Jamie had agreed to help Clint Adams, and not Jim Hickok. That was her condition. She also wanted the Turners away from her brother before they got him killed. After Jamie found Clint and told her what she had overheard, she hurried off to do some shopping so she wouldn't go back to the house empty-handed.

Clint went to find Hickok to tell him that, one way or another, the next two days should tell the tale.

# TWENTY-THREE

"I can't believe you got Jamie to spy on her brother," Hickok said. "She knows that by doing that she's helping me, doesn't she?"

"She doesn't choose to look at it that way, Bill."

They were sitting with Ed Blaine in the Deadline Saloon at their usual table. When Clint entered, Hickok and Blaine were deep in a discussion of campaign business, but they suspended it to hear what Clint had to say.

"She's helping you, then," Hickok said.

"Me and her brother," Clint explained. "She thinks that the Turners are going to get her brother killed."

"Did you tell her that you'd keep her brother safe?" Hickok asked.

"She knows I couldn't promise that."

"And she still agreed to help?"

"Yes."

"I envy this power you have over women, Clint," Hickok said, and Clint frowned, wondering if there was more to that statement than met the eye.

"It seems to me we'd better address ourselves to the information she brought to you," Ed Blaine said.

"Yes," Clint said. "Tutt's getting impatient and nervous, so sometime within the next two days he's going to cut the Turners loose."

"We'd better keep our women on call," Hickok said.

"What women?" Blaine asked.

"Do you want to explain or should I?" Hickok asked Clint.

"You go ahead," Clint said, and Hickok explained their plan for keeping the Turners separated.

"That sounds risky," Blaine said. "If Tutt sends them after Jim, you think two women are going to slow them down?"

"Like I told Jamie," Clint said, "Tutt sent for the Turners, and he's paying them, but that doesn't mean he can control them. I'm betting that those two young fellas don't have too much experience with women. For a chance to go to bed with these ladies we've, uh, employed, I think they'd put off killing Bill—and then we can pull their claws."

"Well, I hope it works."

"It might work," Hickok said, "but if it does it will only keep the Turner brothers alive, not Dave Tutt and Jim Courtwright."

"Jim—" Blaine started to caution, but Hickok didn't let him finish.

"Ed, this has got to come to an end sooner or later. If Tutt sends the Turners after me and we stop them, then I'm going after him."

"And you'll blow the election."

"I don't think so," Hickok said. "People want a lawman who can take care of himself."

Blaine stared at Hickok and asked, "Are you telling me that you actually think that by killing Dave Tutt and Jim Courtwright you can win votes?"

Hickok nodded and said, "A few."

Blaine sat back in his chair and shook his head. "I'm sorry, Jim," he said, "but I can't see it that way."

"What do you mean?"

"I can't go along with winning votes through gunplay or

murder. If you insist on this course of action, I'm going to have to walk away from this campaign.''

Hickok was staring at Blaine and gaping. He had not heard anything after the word *murder*. "Murder?" he asked. "Is that what you call it?"

"What do you call it?"

"Justice, damn it!" Hickok exploded. "Those two betrayed me more than once during the war. I almost lost my life and a few men did because of them. They're a couple of traitors and murderers, and although I was never able to prove it, I've judged them guilty."

Blaine was about to speak when Hickok pushed his chair back and stood up. "If you want to walk away, Ed, then you go ahead," he said, glaring down at the portly ex-newspaperman, "but don't think I'm gonna forget the debt I owe those two just because of this campaign." With that Hickok walked away from the table and left the saloon.

Blaine looked at Clint and said, "What happened here?"

"You said the magic word," Clint said, "*murder*."

"I didn't meant that—"

"Don't tell me; tell Hickok," Clint advised him. "He feels very strongly about Tutt and Courtwright."

"But he's never been able to prove anything."

"He's proven it to himself."

"Is that the kind of lawman he'd be?" Ed Blaine asked, looking shaken. "I guess I don't know him all that well, do I?"

"Ed, maybe neither one of us knows him very well, but I've been a lawman, so let me tell you something I learned from experience. You can't uphold the law strictly by the letter of the law. It's impossible."

"You've taken the law into your own hands while wearing a badge?"

"More than once," Clint said, nodding, "and each time I

was certain I was in the right.''

"What if you weren't?''

"It never came to that,'' Clint said, "because nobody ever proved I wasn't.''

"There, you used the word,'' Blaine said, pointing his finger, *"proved."*

"If we were all sure of ourselves before we acted, Ed, we probably wouldn't need to have lawmen. We could all just do what we thought was right and nobody would question us.''

"You're saying that someone has to have the right to take the law into his own hands.''

"I'm saying that someone has to have the right—and the power—to do what has to be done.''

Blaine sat for a few moments, looking off into space, and then he said, "Look, I'm sorry but I've got to think about this a little.''

"Take your time,'' Clint said. "I want you to make the right decision.''

"The right decision,'' Blaine said, shaking his head. "Even if I decide to stick with him, he may not want to stick with me.''

"Oh, I think the two of you will be able to work it out.''

He stood up and said, "I'll see you later, Clint.''

Clint watched him leave and wondered how many people thought the way he did, that upholding the law was a by-the-book occupation.

There'd be a lot more dead lawmen if that were true.

# TWENTY-FOUR

When Jamie Tutt returned to the boardinghouse, she found Jim Courtwright just where she had left him—in the sitting room.

"Just had to do some shopping," she said nervously, showing the small bag of groceries she'd purchased.

She hurried into the kitchen, hoping that he believed her. As she was putting the groceries away, Courtwright came walking in behind her.

Jim Courtwright was puzzled. In all the time he had known Dave Tutt and lived at this boardinghouse, he could count on one hand the times that Jamie Tutt had spoken to him first. He knew that she didn't like him, even though he couldn't help but like her—and maybe his feelings even went a little deeper than that.

He followed her into the kitchen to find out why she suddenly felt she had to explain her comings and goings to him. "Jamie," Courtwright said, and she turned, surprised by his appearance.

"What are you doing in my kitchen?"

"I was curious," he said, "about where you just came from."

"I told you I was going shopping before I left," she replied. Then she stuck her chin out defiantly and added, "Besides, I don't have to explain myself to you."

"That's what I thought, too," he said, "so now I'm curious about why you did, twice, once before you left and just now as you came back in. Both times you made a point of telling me that you were doing some shopping. Why, Jamie?"

"Look—"

"Did you go somewhere else, too?"

"Of course not," she said, turning her back to him and picking up a potato she'd just bought.

"Then why are you so nervous?"

She slammed the vegetable back down on the table and whirled on him so viciously that he actually backed away from her a step. "You want to know why I'm nervous?" she demanded. "I'll tell you why. My own brother has decided that it's suddenly okay to beat me, and I've got two crazy killers living in my house. I want to get out, Jim!"

"Dave hit you?"

"Never mind, Jim, just never mind . . ." she said, turning away again.

Courtwright grabbed her by the shoulders and turned her around forcefully. "Jamie, you know how I feel about you," he said, looking into her eyes. "You won't have to be afraid of Dave, or the Turners, or anybody, ever again, if you'd just—"

"Let me go, Jim" she said, pulling away. "I'll be fine; just leave me alone."

He backed away from her, saying, "Sure, Jamie, sure, I'll leave you alone. Just remember what I said, all right?"

When she didn't answer, he left the kitchen and walked right into Dave Tutt. "What's wrong, Jim?" Tutt asked. Dave Tutt was a much bigger man than Jim Courtwright, but that didn't stop the smaller man from grabbing Tutt by the arm.

"Jamie says you hit her, Dave," Courtwright said. "I don't want to hear that it happened again, you understand? Don't ever hit her again."

"What?"

"Don't hit her again!"

Tutt stared at Courtwright for a moment, then put a massive hand against his chest, and pushed. Courtwright staggered back, releasing Tutt's arm, and almost fell, regaining his balance at the last moment.

Tutt pointed a finger at Courtwright and said, "Don't tell me what to do to my own sister, Jim. You don't have that right. Nobody does!"

The two men glared at each other for a few tense moments and then Courtwright turned and stormed out of the house before he or Tutt could remember that they were wearing guns.

When Jim Courtwright entered the Deadline later that evening, Clint Adams looked up from his full house and watched the man walk to the bar. Actually, stagger would have been a better description of what he did, and then when he leaned on the bar Clint was sure that he would have fallen over if someone sneezed in that direction.

Jim Courtwright had been drinking for a long time, and the Gunsmith wondered why.

"Full house," he said, showing his cards and raking in his money. "I'll be back a little later, gents."

He pocketed his winnings and walked to the bar to stand next to Courtwright.

"A beer, Joe."

Brewer brought the beer and asked, "How are you doing tonight?"

"Real good," Clint replied, and then he looked at

Courtwright and asked, "How are you doing, Courtwright?"

"Huh?" the other man answered, turning his head and squinting his eyes. "You talking to me?"

"I was."

"What'd you say?"

"I asked you how you were doing?"

"I need a drink."

"Bring my friend a beer, Joe," Clint said because the man didn't need more whiskey.

"How am I?" Courtwright muttered. "How would you feel if you had a fight with your best friend?"

Trouble in Paradise. "That's rough."

"Yeah, rough," Courtwright said. "The man's like a brother to me, but his sister—"

"What?"

Courtwright grabbed the beer like a drowning man and downed half of it.

"What about his sister?"

"Pretty," Courtwright said, "she's pretty."

"Yeah, she is."

"Yeah." Courtwright finished the beer and turned to leave.

"Hey, Jim—" Clint said, putting his hand on the man's arm. Courtwright pulled it away with so much force that he almost fell over. When he righted himself, he glared at Clint with bloodshot eyes.

"Sister or no sister, the man's like a brother to me," he shouted, "so if you and Hickok go after him, you got to go after me, too. Understand?"

"Sure, Jim, sure, I understand. Take it easy."

"Fuck you," Courtwright said and staggered out into the street.

"What was that all about?" Joe Brewer asked.

"Unrequited love, I think," Clint said, putting two and two together and coming up with a man who was in love with his best friend's sister. "And maybe a touch of misplaced loyalty."

# TWENTY-FIVE

Clint left the Deadline Saloon to go back to his hotel, hoping that the morning would bring about some changes in the way things stood at that moment. He particularly hoped that Blaine would be able to reconcile himself to the way Hickok—and he himself—felt the law should be upheld and that the two men would renew their friendship and their business relationship.

Clint felt that Ed Blaine and Hickok needed each other. After Hickok became marshal, they'd be able to part company and go their own ways with no regrets, he hoped.

He had almost reached his hotel when he realized that he had to let the two gals know to be on the alert. He altered his course so he could go to Mandy and Pat's room. He had found out from Mandy that Pat was her roommate, so he knew he'd find one or both of the gals there.

The question was whether or not they'd be alone.

When he knocked on the door, it was opened by Mandy, who leaned on the door and eyed him lasciviously. He wondered if prostitutes did that to all the men they met all the time. She was wearing a revealing nightie and he found himself staring at the firm slopes of her breasts.

"Hello, Mandy," he said. "Am I, uh, interrupting anything?"

"Not much," she said. "I rarely bring my work home with me anyway, Mr. Adams."

"Clint."

"Clint," she said, smiling. "One of the first things I learned in this business was that there's always a room available."

"I just came up to let you know—"

"Why don't you come in?" she invited. "Pat's here and maybe you'd like to say what you have to say to both of us."

"Sure, thanks."

He stepped in past her and she closed the door. There was only one bed in the room, but it was a large one. On it was Pat, the tall, leggy red-haired one who was also wearing a revealing nightgown. Her breasts were probably no smaller than her friend's, but since she was taller, they seemed to be small. Still, they were nice and round and firm and she was very pretty.

"Pat, this is one of the men I told you about," Mandy said, "Clint Adams. Clint, this is my roommate, Patricia Muldoon."

Clint thought that something passed between the women, but he couldn't quite catch all of it.

"Hello," Pat said, smiling and carefully crossing her bare legs. "Call me Pat."

"Hi, Pat."

"He's got something to tell us."

"About the job?"

"It's going to happen within the next couple of days, ladies," Clint said. "I just want to let you know to be ready. Have you got somewhere to take them?"

"We've got rooms," Mandy said, "like I told you. There's always a place."

"Which of you has which?" he asked, out of curiosity.

"I've got the right-handed one," Mandy said, "and Pat's taking the left-handed one. Neither one's a prize, and that's the only way we can tell them apart."

"Okay."

"Are we getting paid enough to handle these two losers, Mandy?" Pat asked, grinning at Clint.

"I don't know . . ." Mandy said, eyeing Clint speculatively.

"We made a deal," Clint reminded her.

"I want a new deal," Pat Muldoon said.

Clint started to respond and then an inkling of what they were talking about dawned on him.

"What kind of a deal are we talking about?" Clint asked, looking at each of them in turn.

"Well," Mandy said, putting her hand on his belt buckle, "we could start with your pants."

He looked at her and remembered turning her down the first time they met.

Looking at Pat's legs, he removed his gunbelt, undid his pants, and let them fall to the floor. Mandy leaned over, snuck her hand into his longjohns, got herself a handful, and pulled out his penis.

"See, Pat," she said breathlessly, "didn't I tell you?"

Pat sat up and, with a swift movement, her nightie was gone. Her breasts were firm and russet-tipped and there was a sprinkle of freckles between them. He looked at her long, lithe legs again and followed them up to her thighs.

When he looked at Mandy, he saw that she, too, had shed her nightie. Her body was full and lush. Clint was not at all averse to striking a new deal with these two ladies.

The new deal struck, Clint returned to his hotel for a well-deserved rest. He was now more than convinced that those two ladies would be able to hold the attention of Ethan and Elmo Turner for as long as was necessary.

As he reached the door to his room, a door opened farther down the hall. Susannah Moore stepped out into the hallway and, hands on hips, regarded him with her head tilted to one side.

"Keeping late hours now, are we?"

"Business, Susannah," he said, "business."

"I'll bet," she said. She reached for her door, closed it, and walked down the hall to stand with him before his.

"Whew!" she said, holding her hand out as if to ward him off. "You smell like you just came from a whorehouse."

"Well, as a matter of fact . . ." he said.

"I don't want to hear the sordid details, Mr. Adams," she said, taking his key and opening his door. "Wait here."

She went into his room and reappeared a few moments later carrying a towel.

"Take this and I'll wait right here for you."

"A towel?"

"You don't think I'm going to let you into bed with me while you reek of other women's perfumes and . . . musk, do you? That understanding I'm not."

She closed his door in his face and he went downstairs to take a bath.

He was in the tub when the door to the room opened and a breeze chilled him. He turned, reached for his gun, and stopped when he saw Susannah approaching the tub, naked.

"What the hell—"

"Cat around all evening with a half dozen whores, will you?" she said, kneeling down by the tub.

"It wasn't a half dozen—"

She dropped a bar of soap into the tub and watched it sink between his legs.

"Now, we'll find out what kind of a man you really are," she said, reaching into the water.

He hoped that he'd still be able to rise to the occasion—and he did.

# TWENTY-SIX

Clint woke feeling more than mild fatigue in his loins, but he'd never complained about that in the past.

"What's going to happen today?" Susannah asked him while she watched him dress. He explained to her his reason for staying with the two whores and she laughed, saying that he should always be in such demand with the ladies.

"Tell a woman no," he had said, "and she wants you all the more."

She slapped him lightly because she knew that he was also referring to her and then they made love again.

Now, as he dressed, he said, "I don't know what will happen today, Susannah, but we've got to be ready for anything."

"Well, I like Jim Hickok," she said, rising from the bed and padding naked to him, "but do me a favor; don't think about giving up your life for his."

"Jesus," he said, staring at her, "that thought never entered my mind."

James Butler Hickok rose early that morning so that he could clean his guns. Hs wanted to be sure that, if he needed them that day or the next, they would be in perfect working order. He'd seen too many men die because their guns would misfire or jam. He swore he would never die that way. The only way he would accept death was at the hands of a man who was faster and better than he with a gun.

To date, he'd only seen one man who might fit that description, and he doubted that he and Clint Adams, the Gunsmith, would ever draw on each other. In fact, he didn't mind admitting that he would be afraid to draw against Adams since the Gunsmith was the only man Hickok had ever seen whose speed matched his own.

Adams was his friend first, however, and Wild Bill Hickok's friendships were instantaneous and lasting—which was why he was going to use the early part of this day to patch things up with Ed Blaine.

The rest of the day would be used in winning an election—and staying alive.

Ed Blaine felt foolish that morning. His attitude the previous evening had been almost prudish and he wanted to apologize to Clint Adams and Jim Hickok. He hoped that he would also be able to continue managing his campaign for marshal. He had signed on to get him into office, and once that was done, it was up to Hickok how he wanted to conduct his term.

He left his room to go to Hickok's to invite him to breakfast.

Hickok and Blaine met in the hall and settled their differences over breakfast.

Breakfast at the Tutt boardinghouse was strained, but afterward Courtwright cornered Dave Tutt and made his peace with him.

"I know how you feel about Jamie, Jim," Tutt said, "and I did hit her but once. I'm sorry I did, too, because it's the only time in our lives I ever touched her. It won't happen again."

"That's your business, Dave," Courtwright said. "I just wanted to make sure we were still friends."

"Oh, sure we are."

"And I want to tell you that whatever you decide about Hickok I'll back you all the way."

"I appreciate that, Jim."

"When are you going to cut the Turners loose?"

"The election's next week, but I don't think I'll wait that long. If he wins, I don't want the Turners to be gunning down a lawman."

"They wouldn't mind."

"But I would. That would bring too much heat down on us. No, I think I'll let them loose today and let them pick the best time to make their move. They may not be very smart, but they know when they can take somebody and when they can't."

"I hope so."

"Don't worry about it, Jim. I'll let them know that Hickok should be taken care of today or tomorrow."

"All right," Courtwright said with very little enthusiasm.

"Jim, I really do appreciate this—"

"Never mind," Courtwright said. "I'll be around if you need me, Dave."

"Good."

Courtwright turned to leave so quietly that Jamie didn't hear him coming. She froze in panic on the steps, where she'd been listening, but Courtwright never looked her way. Sweating, she watched as he went straight to the front door and left the house. She let her breath out, turned, and went up the steps. She had to let the Turners know that breakfast for the house was over, and they could come down now and have theirs.

After that, she had to find Clint Adams.

Dave Tutt joined the Turner boys while they were eating

their breakfast. He told Jamie to leave the room. She did, but stopped outside the door in the sitting room to listen.

"You gonna eat?" Elmo asked Tutt, eyeing the food in the center of the table as if he were afraid there wouldn't be enough for him and his brother.

"No, no," Tutt said, "it's all yours. I just want to talk to you."

"Talk," Ethan said.

"I want you to find Hickok today and—between today and tomorrow—take your best shot at him."

"What if he sees us and comes after us?" Elmo asked.

"That'd be even better," Tutt said, and then something occurred to him. "You might even pass a rumor around town that will bring him to me."

"What kind of rumor?"

"Tell people that you heard that his woman, Susannah Moore, slept with me."

Elmo looked at Tutt and said, "Did she?"

"Yes."

"Shouldn't be messing with someone else's woman," Ethan commented.

"Never mind that," Tutt said, shaking his head, "just pass it around. When he hears that, he's bound to come after me and that will be when you can take him."

"We'll decide when we can take him," Ethan Turner said around a mouthful of ham and eggs.

"All right, just pass the word and wait for your opening."

Elmo looked at Ethan, then back at Tutt, and said, "Can we finish eating first?"

# TWENTY-SEVEN

When Clint Adams started into the hotel dining room, he saw Hickok and Blaine sitting together, eating and talking animatedly. He backed away quickly, before they could see him, and left the hotel to look for somewhere else to eat breakfast. He figured the two men could use the time together to set their relationship straight.

As he stepped out into the street, he saw Jamie Tutt across the street, looking around nervously. She was obviously trying to decide whether to enter the hotel. When she saw him, she started to wave, then caught herself, and put both arms at her sides awkwardly.

He inclined his head toward an alley, hoping that she would get the idea, and then started that way. He entered the alley first and had to wait a few moments before Jamie joined him nervously.

"Dave is at the house with the Turners, but Jim Courtwright is around," she said, explaining her nervousness.

"What's the matter, Jamie?"

"I heard Jim and Dave talking this morning. Jim told him that he would back him all the way."

"I expected that. What else?"

"Dave just told the Turners to be ready today or tomorrow and to take their best shot. He also told them to pass a rumor that Dave and Susannah Moore slept together. That isn't true, is it, Clint?''

"I'm afraid it is, Jamie."

She looked annoyed and said, "Even my own brother! What do you men see in her?" She held her hand up then and said, "Don't answer that."

"You'd better get back to the house, Jamie. Thanks for the information."

She grabbed his hands and said, "Just don't get yourself killed, Clint, not even for a friend."

As she left him there, he couldn't help thinking that people were giving him credit for being much more noble than he was.

He went directly back to the hotel and walked to the dining room. He hoped that Hickok and Blaine had made up by now because he had to join them.

"Sorry to interrupt you," he said, sitting down, "but we have to talk."

Both men stared at him as if he were crazy and Hickok said, "What are you talking about?"

"You fellas bury the hatchet?"

"Oh, yeah, sure," Hickok said.

"Sure thing," Blaine said.

Clint waved to a waiter and, when he came over, asked for another coffee cup and another pot of coffee.

"You're not eating breakfast?"

"No time," Clint said. "I just talked to Jamie."

"The Turners?" Hickok asked.

Clint nodded. "Tutt's turned them loose," Clint said. "They're to use their own judgment about when to take you, but it's got to be done today or tomorrow."

"He wants it done before you win the election," Ed Blaine said and Clint looked at him in surprise.

"Right," he said, accepting the pot of coffee and extra cup from the waiter.

"I'll stick with you all day today and tomorrow—" Clint started, but Hickok stopped him.

"You can follow me all you want, Clint, but I ain't about to walk around with you as my bodyguard. Ed and I have some campaigning to do and I'm not going to change my schedule for the Turners. Whenever they make their move, I'll be ready."

"What about Ed?"

"Don't worry about me."

"Ed doesn't carry a gun."

"I'll get one," Blaine said.

"When they try for you, he could get hurt," Clint went on, "or killed."

"Hey!" Blaine shouted, and when both men looked at him, he said, "Can we stop talking about me as if I weren't here, please? Why don't you ask me what I think?"

"What do you think?"

"I'll be all right," Blaine insisted. "Don't worry about me."

"Bill—"

"Just lay back, Clint, and keep your eyes open. It'll be fine."

Frowning, Blaine asked, "Whatever happened with these two girls you've got lined up? How is that going to work? Are they going to keep these two men in bed all day?"

"That is just a contingency plan," Clint said, avoiding the man's eyes. He wasn't sure that the money they were paying Mandy and Pat wasn't just going to go to waste. It had seemed like a good idea at the time, but now it just didn't seem feasible. What were the girls supposed to do, follow the Turners around and drop their clothes if the two men went for their guns?

"We knew it might not work when we talked to them," Hickok said, covering for Clint. "Look, fellas, it'll work out. I cleaned my guns this morning." As if that settled the whole matter Wild Bill Hickok stood up and said, ''Come on, Ed, we've got a meeting at the town hall.''

"Right," Blaine said.

Clint started to lift his cup to his lips and then realized that he'd have to follow Hickok. "Ah, shit," he said and hurriedly rose to follow the two men out.

# TWENTY-EIGHT

Clint followed Hickok and Blaine to their campaign meetings until late afternoon and saw both Turners every time. He did not approach them and was impressed by Hickok's restraint in not approaching them. Ed Blaine, on the other hand, was obviously a little jumpy and trying his best to hide it. Also present, watching eagerly for some trouble to write about, was Colonel Nichols.

Colonel George Ward Nichols began attending Wild Bill Hickok's campaign speeches for wont of something else to write about, and when he noticed the appearance of the two Turner brothers, plus that of Clint Adams, he knew that something big was in the offing.

Happily, the Colonel knew that he would not be writing about campaign speeches for very much longer.

Dave Tutt stayed away from Hickok's campaign speeches and meetings, but his instructions to Elmo and Ethan were that they were to be seen everywhere that Hickok was. With a little luck, Hickok would get spooked and challenge them, but even if that didn't happen, Tutt knew Hickok would be dead within the next two days, and then he and Jamie and Jim Courtwright could go back to living a normal life without the threat of Wild Bill Hickok hanging over their heads.

Campaign promises went right over Elmo and Ethan Turner's heads. The only promises they knew anything about

145

were the promises of money in return for their killing some-one. They had done it many times before, usually to lesser men than Wild Bill Hickok, but they never rushed into it. They always waited until they were sure it could be done cleanly and quickly.

Waiting was nothing new to them, but listening to Hic-kok's speeches and promises was giving them a headache.

At each meeting, Ed Blaine stood off to the side, listening carefully to Hickok's words and scanning the crowd to see if his words were having the desired effect. If they weren't, then he'd make a slight change in the speech for the next time.

At each meeting, however, he was aware of the presence of the Turners, and Nichols, and Clint, and was wondering when all of this would come together, like a fuse coming together with a stick of dynamite.

He started to think of ways of defusing things.

At a meeting later in the day the cast of characters was the same, except for Ed Blaine, who was missing. Clint Adams noticed the glaring absence of the campaign manager and, after the meeting, asked Hickok where Ed Blaine was.

Hickok shrugged and said, "He had some other business to take care of."

Both Hickok and Clint left the school where this particular meeting had been conducted and saw the Turners standing outside, watching and waiting.

"Clint," Hickok said, "we know they won't make a move while we're together."

"What are you suggesting?" Clint asked. "That I go and hide someplace?"

"That would make things easier," Hickok said. "They'd go ahead and make their try and I'd kill both of them."

Clint shook his head. "That would still leave Dave Tutt."

"Then maybe I ought to just go and kill him," Hickok suggested.

Clint didn't think that was a good idea, but he had no counter suggestion for a way to solve the Tutt-Hickok feud. They started walking toward the center of town with the Turners following at a respectable distance.

"Do you know about Dave Tutt and Susannah?" Hickok asked suddenly.

"Yes," Clint said, "I do, but there's something else you ought to know."

"About you and Susannah?"

"Yes," Clint said, surprised.

"I know all about that, Clint," Hickok said. "That doesn't bother me."

"But the fact that she went with Dave Tutt does?"

"Tutt's my enemy, and you're my friend," Hickok said. "That's the difference."

"You're not planning to go after him for that, are you?"

"When and if I decide to go after Tutt, it'll be for that and more, much, much more."

Clint, recognizing that his friend's ego had been bruised, wondered what was going on inside Wild Bill Hickok's head. "Where are you headed now?"

"I'm supposed to meet Ed at the Deadline."

"And then what?"

"I don't know," Hickok said. "Maybe then I'll go and see Dave Tutt."

"Bill—"

"Then again, maybe not."

"I'm going to hang back a bit, Bill," Clint said, coming to a stop.

"What are you up to?"

"I'll just see you later."

Clint stopped walking and watched as Hickok continued on to the Deadline.

The Turners, seeing that Clint Adams had stopped walking, became momentarily confused and stopped following. From farther back, Jim Courtwright watched, knowing that if they continued, they'd have to walk past Clint Adams and Tutt had warned them not to get distracted by him.

Tutt had sent him to observe from a distance and Courtwright watched with concern to see how the Turners handled the situation. If they killed Adams, Tutt had told them, and not Wild Bill Hickok, they would not get paid.

Finally, they crossed the street to avoid Clint and continued walking toward the Deadline.

That was when the Gunsmith got behind them.

# TWENTY-NINE

Ed Blaine left the room of Mandy Roberts and Pat Muldoon and started to the Deadline to meet Hickok. He didn't like going behind the back of Clint Adams like this, but Hickok said it was the only way to resolve this thing with Dave Tutt.

And Ed Blaine figured the best chance Hickok had of getting elected was to do that.

Moments after Ed Blaine left their room, Mandy and Pat left and headed for the Deadline. They were dressed to turn heads, with gowns cut low over their firm breasts and ending above their well-turned ankles, and the heads they were after sat squarely on the skinny shoulders of Ethan and Elmo Turner.

Jim Courtwright went to Dave Tutt's boardinghouse to report on what he had seen, and so was not within sight of the Deadline when Mandy Roberts and Pat Muldoon entered, cornering their prey.

The Deadline was not crowded at this time of the afternoon. Everyone present seemed to be a part of the impending confrontation.

Bill Hickok and Ed Blaine were seated together at a back table. Clint Adams was standing at the bar with a mug of beer in hand. Ethan and Elmo Turner had taken a table across the room from Hickok. Mandy and Pat had just entered, to the surprise of Clint Adams. Joe Brewer, the bartender, knew that trouble was brewing.

Clint watched, puzzled, as Mandy and Pat approached the Turners' table and sat down. He was wondering what had possessed the two prostitutes to do this at this particular time, and when he looked at Hickok and Ed Blaine, he knew the answer. He also knew why Ed Blaine had missed that last meeting.

The Turner brothers were obviously pleased with the attention they were getting from the women, and they were suitably impressed by the amount of bosom each woman was rubbing against them. Both women had their hands beneath the table as well, and it didn't take much to figure out what they were doing.

Before long, the women stood up and, after just the tiniest bit of cajoling, the Turners stood and followed them out of the saloon.

Clint put his beer down and walked to the doors. He watched as Mandy and Pat took Ethan and Elmo toward their own room where, according to Mandy, they rarely—if ever—did their business. He walked to Hickok and Blaine and said, "You must have paid them quite a bit to get them to take those two to their own room."

Blaine looked helplessly at Hickok, and it was plain whose idea it was.

"Bill?"

Hickok stood up and said, "Stay here, Ed."

"Bill, don't do this—" Clint started to say, but Hickok cut him off.

"This has to end, Clint," he said, "and this is the only way. Why don't you stay here with Ed?"

"I'll tag along."

"Don't get in my way," Hickok said, pinning the

Gunsmith with a cold, hard stare. "You're my friend, Clint, but I'm warning you, don't get in my way!"

Colonel Nichols had tired of attending Hickok's campaign speeches and gone back to his hotel earlier. From his hotel room Nichols could look out his window at the Deadline Saloon, and he had gotten into the habit of doing so at all hours. After he saw Hickok go in, he'd returned to his room to watch and wait. Now, after seeing them all go in—Hickok, the twin gunmen, Clint Adams, Blaine and the two women—he saw the women come out with the gunmen and lead them away. He watched them until he knew which building they were going into. After that, Hickok came out and started walking toward the end of town where Dave Tutt's boardinghouse was.

Nichols was sure that Hickok was going after Tutt while the two women kept the gunmen busy.

There was no story in that, but if the two gunmen knew what was going on and went to help Tutt, there'd be a hell of a shoot-out and a hell of a story to go with it.

Nichols, moving faster than he had ever moved before, left his room.

Clint walked out of the saloon after Hickok and stared after the man. Wild Bill would certainly be able to take care of Dave Tutt and Jim Courtwright as well. Instead of following him, maybe he would be better off making sure the Turners didn't change their minds.

Of course, the girls could handle that part without his help.

Still undecided about which way to go, Clint saw Colonel Nichols come charging out of his hotel and run across the street. It took him a moment to realize where he was going, and by then it was too late to stop him. Not wanting to have any gunplay around the women, he decided to follow Hickok and back him up just in case the Turners showed up.

Which, if Nichols had his way, was exactly what would happen.

When Nichols found the building the two women had taken the gunmen to, he saw the stairway leading up to a door. Since the hardware shop beneath it was closed, he went up the steps and knocked on the door. When nobody answered, he used his impressive bulk and forced it open, feeling a rush of excitement as he did.

As he burst into the room the tableau that faced him was comical. Both of the skinny killers had their pants down around their ankles, but their gunbelts were still riding their naked hips. Kneeling in front of one was the willowy redhead. The other brother had a chunky blonde kneeling on the floor before him, and she was rolling his penis between her creamy white breasts and moaning appreciatively.

"What the hell—" the blonde said because she was the one with her mouth free.

"I've got something to tell these gentlemen that they'll be very interested in, ladies," Nichols said. "I'm sorry to break up the party, but . . ."

# THIRTY

By the time Clint reached the boardinghouse, the front door was wide open, having apparently been kicked in. Inside, he heard raised voices and, among them, a woman's.

Jamie Tutt. As he entered, he heard her saying, "You can't do this, Jim Hickok!"

"Do what?" Hickok asked.

Clint entered the sitting room and saw Hickok facing Jamie Tutt, and behind her, her brother Dave Tutt. Actually, Dave wasn't standing behind her so much as she was standing in front of him, between him and Hickok. Clint wondered where Jim Courtwright was.

"You can't gun him down in our home," Jamie was saying. "He isn't even wearing a gun."

"That can be fixed," Hickok said. "Get a gun, Tutt, and meet me outside. I'll be waiting."

Jamie looked past Hickok at Clint and said, "Clint, do something."

"All I can do, Jamie," Clint said with an apologetic shrug, "is make sure it goes off fairly. Where's Jim Courtwright?"

"Oh, I don't know—"

"All right, Hickok," Tutt said, pushing his sister aside, "I'll be out as soon as I strap on my gun. This is gonna be a pleasure."

Hickok didn't speak to Tutt; he simply turned and stalked past Clint and out of the house.

"You backing him, Adams?"

"Not against you, Tutt," Clint said, "but if Courtwright or the Turners show up, I'll take a hand."

"Then you're as good as dead, too."

"We'll see," Clint said and left.

When they were alone, Jamie faced Dave and said, "So it's finally come to this."

"Shut up," Tutt said. Suddenly, he looked nervous. "Where the hell are those blasted brothers?"

Jamie frowned and asked, "Where's Courtwright?"

"I know where he is," Tutt said, strapping on his gun, "it's the Turners I'm worried about."

Jamie knew now that her brother wasn't so much worried about the Turners as he was worried doing without them.

She didn't know her brother at all.

Outside, Clint went and stood with Hickok. "We're going to have company soon," Clint said.

"What are you talking about?"

"Your friend Nichols is about to interrupt Mandy, Pat, and the Turners to tell them what they're missing."

"Why would he do that?"

"Come on, Bill," Clint said. "This is the chance Nichols has been waiting for. You against Tutt, Courtwright, and the Turners. It's the stuff that legends are made of."

Looking down the street, Hickok said, "All of a sudden I'm not so sure I want to be a legend."

"All right," Tutt said, adjusting his belt and looking up, "we're going to have to do this ourselves."

"What are you talking about?" Jamie asked. All she saw was the ceiling, but she knew there had to be more to it than that.

"Stay inside, Jamie, do you hear?" Dave Tutt said. "Stay inside."

"Sure, Dave," Jamie said, "sure."

The Turner boys pulled their pants back up over their skinny legs and lit out, leaving two puzzled and very naked girls behind. Nichols stared at both women and wondered if they were already paid for.

"Don't even think about it, old timer," the blonde said, facing him with her hands on her hips and her full, succulent breasts thrust toward him.

The redhead laughed, assumed a similar pose with her legs wide open, and said, "You'd never survive it."

Face burning, Nichols took out after the Turners, deciding that he really wouldn't have had the time to spare, anyway.

The two women exchanged glances and wondered if they were going to have to give the money back.

Ed Blaine left the Deadline Saloon and saw the Turner boys rushing down the street with the portly Colonel Nichols hurrying behind them. He decided it was time for him to join the party as more than a spectator.

"Here he comes," Clint said, looking at the front door of the boardinghouse.

"Here they come," Hickok said, looking down the street behind the Gunsmith. "I'll have to take care of them first."

"No time for that," Clint said. "I'll take care of the twins."

"You gonna be able to handle them?"

"You just worry about Tutt," Clint said, "and don't forget about Jim Courtwright. He's got to be around here someplace."

''Good luck,'' Hickok said, starting his move toward the house and Dave Tutt.

''We'll need it,'' Clint said, and he moved to meet the Turners.

# THIRTY-ONE

From his position on the roof of the boardinghouse, Courtwright had his choice. He could have picked off Hickok or Adams with his rifle, but that was to be a last resort, only if Tutt should find himself facing either of them without the benefit of the Turners.

And the Turners were here, now.

Courtwright aimed his rifle in their direction and settled down to watch and wait.

When Tutt stepped out of the boardinghouse, he was relieved to see the Turners approaching, until he realized that Adams was moving to intercept them, which left Hickok free to face him . . . and Jim Courtwright.

He and Courtwright would have to handle it themselves, then—which was probably the way it would have to end.

Ethan and Elmo stopped when they saw Clint Adams standing in their path.

"What do we do, Ethan?" Elmo asked.

Elmo, remembering the deal they had made with Dave Tutt, said, "If we kill him, we don't get paid."

Ethan looked past Clint Adams and saw Wild Bill Hickok approaching the boardinghouse, where Dave Tutt was standing on the steps.

"Elmo, if we don't kill him, Hickok will kill Tutt, and then we won't get paid, anyway."

Elmo considered his brother's words and decided that they made sense. "I guess we better kill him, then," he said, and the brothers started walking again.

As Clint watched them walk purposefully toward him, he knew they had made their decision. In order to help Dave Tutt, they were going to have to go through him and that's just what they intended to do. Together.

History showed that together the Turner brothers were unbeatable. Plans to separate them, however, had gone awry, thanks to Colonel Nichols, and so now the Gunsmith found himself facing the two deadly killers.

Hickok concentrated on Dave Tutt and put his peripheral vision to work. As much as he wanted to turn around and check on Clint Adams, he resisted.

"This showdown has been a long time coming, Tutt," he called out.

Tutt stepped down off the steps and began walking to meet him. "I should have killed you a long time ago, Hickok," he said. Tutt was moving just far enough away from the house to keep Hickok in Courtwright's view. Letting Hickok get too close to the house would have taken him out of range of the other man's gun.

"You never saw the day you could kill me, Tutt," Hickok said, "unless it was from behind."

"Today's the day, Hickok," Tutt retorted, "and you'll see that it won't come from behind." From above maybe, Tutt thought, but not from behind.

"Stop there!" The Turners stopped in response to the Gunsmith's command.

"You have to get out of our way," Ethan said.

"Or we'll have to kill you," Elmo finished.

"You mean you'll try."

"Mister," Ethan said, "we can take anybody as long as we're together."

"Anybody," Elmo agreed.

"Not this time, boys," Clint said, shaking his head, eyeing them with more confidence than he felt. Not today . . . he hoped.

Jamie Tutt looked out the front window and saw Hickok facing her brother, and something gnawed at her. Upon reflection, she did not think that her brother would have the courage to face Hickok alone. He wouldn't do it, not without Jim Courtwright to back him up, at least.

And that's when she remembered her brother's momentary glance upward—not at the ceiling or at heaven—but toward the roof! She grabbed the nearest thing—a whiskey bottle— and hurried up the steps.

Nichols couldn't believe his eyes. This was more than he had ever hoped for when he came west. He sat down right in the street with his notebook in his lap and began writing as fast as the words came to him.

> There was Clint Adams, the famous Gunsmith, facing the twin killers, two of the fastest guns in the west, while Wild Bill Hickok faced down his archenemy, the master gunman Dave Tutt.

He put his pencil down and watched in rapt attention to see what would happen next.

# THIRTY-TWO

Everything that happened next went down in Colonel George Ward Nichols's little notebook.

The Turner brothers stood so that there was no danger of their arms getting tangled. They did stand close to each other.

To Colonel Nichols, they each seemed to move faster than the eye could follow. He wrote: *I had never seen anything move so fast in my life . . . until the Gunsmith drew!*

Clint saw them move and knew that they were fast. Even as he drew and shot Elmo, he knew that they deserved the reputation they had built up. This was a new experience for them, however, and Ethan did not react well or wisely. When he heard his brother cry out in pain, he paused just long enough for the Gunsmith to fire again. The bullet struck Ethan where the previous one had struck Elmo, on the left side of the chest. His shots had come so close together that the Turner brothers died as they had lived most of their lives . . . together.

Wild Bill Hickok heard the shots, but kept his eyes on Dave Tutt. Suddenly, he knew that he could clearly outdraw Tutt and he didn't want to.

"Hold on a minute, Dave," Hickok said.

"What the hell—" Tutt said, frowning.

"I think you're better with your hands than you are with a

gun, Dave,'' Hickok said, dropping both guns to the ground.
''This will give you a fighting chance.''

Dave Tutt looked down at Hickok's guns and then at the
man's face.

''All right!'' he said in agreement, because he knew he
could tear Hickok apart with his bare hands. He undid his
gunbelt, dropped it to the ground, and said, ''Let's go.''

From the roof Courtwright saw the guns of both men hit the
ground and his mouth dropped open in surprise. Hand to
hand, Hickok wouldn't have a chance against Dave Tutt. The
man was crazy. And as good as dead.

Clint, satisfied that the Turner boys were dead and no
longer a threat, turned to see if Hickok needed help and saw
the two men warily circling each other.

He holstered his gun and settled down to watch.

Tutt, confident that he was much stronger than Hickok,
was the first to stop circling and charge forward. Hickok, the
faster and lighter of the two, easily sidestepped the charge
and, extending his foot, sent Tutt sprawling into the dirt.

''Clumsy.''

Tutt got quickly to his feet and said, ''I'm gonna break
your back.''

''You're gonna try.''

Tutt moved forward again, more cautiously this time, arms
held out from his sides. His intention was plain. He was
hoping to wrap those powerful, thickly muscled arms around
Hickok and squeeze the life out of him.

Hickok backed away from Tutt, causing the man to quick-
en his pace involuntarily. Leaning forward, Tutt was
slightly off balance, and when he grabbed for Hickok, Wild
Bill used that against him and sent him sprawling again with a
quick move.

Tutt leaped to his feet this time and angrily charged Hickok again. This time when Hickok sidestepped he struck Tutt behind the ear with his right fist, hastening his trip to the ground.

Tutt rolled over, sat up, and shook his head in an attempt to clear it.

"Let's call it off, Tutt," Wild Bill Hickok said, "the whole feud."

"And what do I have to do?"

"Admit that you were a traitor during the war and that you almost caused my death."

"Damn you, Hickok," Tutt shouted, and he moved faster than Hickok anticipated. Suddenly, Hickok was in Tutt's grasp, within the circle of his arms, and he felt the pressure increasing. His breath began to come painfully and spots began to appear before his eyes. He knew that if he didn't do something, Dave Tutt was going to break his back—and kill him.

Using the only weapon he had, Hickok drew his head back and then jerked it forward. His forehead struck Tutt squarely in the nose, breaking it. Tutt cried out in pain, backstepped, and released his hold on Hickok.

Free, Hickok followed up his advantage quickly. He moved in on Tutt and hit him quickly three times, left-right-left, dropping him to the ground, right by his gunbelt. Hickok took some deep breaths, then walked over to where he'd left his guns. He bent over, retrieved them, and tucked them into his belt.

Clint Adams kept his eyes on Tutt while Hickok picked up his guns. He saw Tutt lift his head, blood dripping from his nose to the dirt, and saw the man reach for his gun.

"Bill, look out!"

Suddenly Tutt shouted, "Now!" as his hand closed around the butt of his gun. Hickok whirled around and drew easily, using one gun. He fired a single shot, ending his feud with Dave Tutt the only way it could have ended.

In Nichols's notebook it was described this way:

> *When Dave Tutt drew, his speed was like lightning, but the legendary Wild Bill Hickok drew both of his guns and fired each one time. Tutt staggered and bravely sought to fire back at his enemy, but his blood was deserting him and with it his strength.*
>
> *The Tutt-Hickok feud was over.*

The only bit of truth was in the last line.

Ed Blaine walked over to where Colonel Nichols was seated and nudged him with his foot.

"In a minute," Nichols said.

"Come on, Nichols," Blaine said. "Stand up."

Nichols finished a line, looked up at Blaine, and then struggled to his feet. "What's your problem, Blaine?"

"You are," Blaine said. "You set part of this up, Nichols. We had the Turners out of it."

"It makes a better story this way, Blaine," Nichols said, "doesn't it?"

"Almost," Blaine said, "except that it needs a new ending."

Nichols laughed and said, "One which you intend to supply?"

"You bet," Blaine said, and while Nichols continued to laugh, Ed Blaine drew back his fist and crashed it into the other man's face. Nichols dropped his notebook to the ground and quickly followed it, landing face down. He raised his head and blinked incredulously.

"The end," Blaine said.

Puzzled as to why Tutt had shouted just before drawing, Hickok kept his gun out and looked around cautiously until, looking up, he spotted Jamie Tutt on the roof. She was holding a bottle in her hand, and draped over the side of the roof was Jim Courtwright.

Hickok turned and saw Clint Adams walking toward him. Looking past the Gunsmith, he saw both Turner brothers lying in the street and, beyond them, Colonel George Ward Nichols, sitting in the street, scribbling madly in his notebook.

When Clint reached him, they both put their guns away and Hickok said, "It's over."

"I guess it is," Clint said.

They were both wrong. It had only just begun.

# EPILOGUE

"It wasn't over?" Hartman asked.

During the story they had moved to Clint's hotel room, bringing a bottle of whiskey and two glasses with them. Clint sat on the bed and Rick Hartman in a wooden chair.

"It had just started," Clint said wearily. "When word got around about what had happened, it was blown all out of proportion. Some stories had it that Bill and I had gunned down a dozen men. The worst part was that a New York paper sent a reporter to write about Bill and me. I avoided the man, but Bill was depicted as the hero of the plains. He started to take it seriously and took to dressing the part. He discarded his buckskins and began to wear a fancy coat and a purple waistband into which he tucked his two colts. Sometimes he even wore a lined cape."

"Jesus," Hartman said. "What about the election? Did Hickok win?"

"He won that hands down and afterward both Ed Blaine and I left town. I didn't want to be around when would-be gunmen started coming out of the woodwork for a shot at the hero of the plains."

"Well, he lasted a long time, didn't he?"

"Not nearly long enough," Clint said, reaching for the bottle on the table, only to find it empty.

"I've had enough, anyway," he said, dropping the empty

bottle on the floor where it rolled until it struck the wall beneath the window.

Clint stood up, walked to the window, and pulled aside the curtain. Dim, early morning light sneaked into the room. "Sun's about to come up."

"What happened to the others, Clint? Susannah Moore, Jamie Tutt."

"Far as I know Jamie stayed and ran the boardinghouse. Jim Courtright left town the following day. Susannah was still there when I left. Bill and I never talked about her whenever we met after that."

"And Blaine?"

"I think I saw his name on some newspaper articles after that, but I lost track of him."

Clint stepped away from the window and ran his hands over his face. "I'm going to get some sleep."

"Clint, I know we've talked all night, but I've got one more question."

"Go ahead."

Whatever happened to Nichols and his notebooks? I have to say that I've never heard of the man. If his stories had been published—"

"Nichols was a good writer," Clint said, "but he didn't have much of a memory. He had to get everything down on paper as fast as he could."

Clint walked over to his bed, bent over, and reached underneath. From a saddlebag he withdrew six or eight small notebooks and tossed them on the bed.

"Just before they loaded his gear on the stage, I liberated these."

Hartman stood up, moved to the bed, and picked one of the books. He opened it and peered intently at the scribblings on the page. He picked up some of the others. "I can't even read this."

"Nichols could have," Clint said, indicating the notebooks, "if he had taken them with him. I got them all, though, and he was never able to duplicate everything he wrote. He tried one or two stories, but they just weren't any good. I don't know what happened to him, then, except that his son told me he died."

Hartman dropped the notebooks back on the bed and faced Clint. "Why did you keep these?"

Clint looked at his friend and said, "I really don't know, Rick, but sometimes I take them out and read them, and I wonder if they had ever gotten printed, could things have been worse for me?"

"I guess things could always be worse, Clint," Rick Hartman said. After a moment's thought, Clint simply nodded.

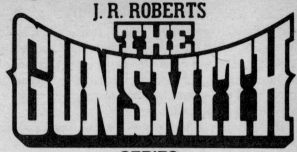

# J. R. ROBERTS
# THE GUNSMITH

## SERIES

Prices may be slightly higher in Canada.